"Is there anything you want me to do?"

It wasn't in Cheyenne to just stand around doing nothing. Besides, if she kept busy, she wouldn't feel tempted by her partner, which at the moment, she was.

"Why don't you just make yourself comfortable?" Jefferson offered.

"Besides that."

Jefferson's smile widened as his eyes washed over her. "Nothing that can bear repeating in mixed company." And then he caught himself. "I shouldn't have even said that."

"Don't worry, I won't hold it against you."

The remark tempted him. "So what will you hold against me?"

Heaven help her but her heart began to pound really hard and breathing grew a good deal harder to regulate.

"What do you want me to hold against you?"

His eyes were already making love to her.

"Guess," he said to her.

With that, he took her into his arms and ever so slowly, he brought his lips down to hers. The growing hunger within him seemed to just explode in his veins, all but consuming every last bit of him.

Dear Reader,

You are holding in your hands a book I wasn't at all sure I could do justice to. You have to understand that I have been writing and making up stories ever since I was eleven years old. This year, I fell victim to long COVID not once, not twice, but three times and suddenly, never mind the story, my mind had gone MIA. However, I refused to give up.

I don't know if I mentioned it previously (I probably did because I have a habit of repeating myself even when my mind is clear) but I am Polish. Polish women are exceedingly stubborn and we refuse to give up. EVER. I knew I had a serial killer story in me somewhere and although it took me longer to create and put down, I was positive that I could. Searching for it not only kept me sane, it also helped me recall all the fundamentals I always held near and dear to my heart (yes, writing about serial killers, doing love scenes and writing dialogue that I prayed would entertain my reader). If this story doesn't work for you, please don't let me know until I manage to write something you do enjoy reading.

Until then, I do thank you for reading and from the bottom of my heart, I wish you someone to love who loves you back. (Thank God I have someone like that. I don't know what I would have done without him.)

With love,

Marie Ferrarella

CAVANAUGH JUSTICE: COLD CASE SQUAD

Marie Ferrarella

HARLEQUIN®
ROMANTIC SUSPENSE™

Recycling programs
for this product may
not exist in your area.

ISBN-13: 978-1-335-59391-7

Cavanaugh Justice: Cold Case Squad

Copyright © 2024 by Marie Rydzynski-Ferrarella

Harlequin Enterprises ULC
22 Adelaide St. West, 41st Floor
Toronto, Ontario M5H 4E3, Canada
www.Harlequin.com

Printed in U.S.A.

USA TODAY bestselling and RITA® Award–winning author **Marie Ferrarella** has written more than three hundred books for Harlequin, some under the name Marie Nicole. Her romances are beloved by fans worldwide. Visit her website, marieferrarella.com.

Books by Marie Ferrarella

Harlequin Romantic Suspense

Cavanaugh Justice

Cavanaugh Vanguard
Cavanaugh Cowboy
Cavanaugh's Missing Person
Cavanaugh Stakeout
Cavanaugh in Plain Sight
Cavanaugh Justice: The Baby Trail
Cavanaugh Justice: Serial Affair
Cavanaugh Justice: Deadly Chase
Cavanaugh Justice: Up Close and Deadly
Cavanaugh Justice: Detecting a Killer
Cavanaugh Justice: Cold Case Squad

The Coltons of New York

Colton's Unusual Suspect

Visit the Author Profile page at Harlequin.com for more titles.

THIS BOOK IS DEDICATED

TO

PATIENCE BLOOM

WITH A GREAT DEAL OF LOVE AND THANKS

FOR BEING SO KIND AND PATIENT

AND FOR MAKING ME FEEL

LIKE THE LUCKIEST WRITER

ON THE FACE OF THE EARTH

Prologue

You never thought that I would ever amount to anything, did you, Aunt Lily? the man asked sharply, his voice as taunting as he had once felt his aunt's had sounded. An ugly smile curved his mouth. *Well, I certainly fooled you, didn't I? The kid you always referred to as being such a big loser didn't turn out to be a loser after all, did he?*

Jon Murphy regarded the face of the woman in the picture on his desk.

He felt that the face was actually looking back at him. He could almost read her thoughts.

It was a big deal for him, keeping that framed photograph right there in front of him. There were times when he would have been a lot happier just hurling it, frame and all, across the room—if not into the garbage altogether.

But he knew that he needed the photograph. One, because he didn't want to answer a lot of questions about what had happened to it—people were incredibly nosy—and two, because it reminded him of his purpose and what he was doing here in the first place. Not in the classroom, but on earth.

His handsome face darkened as he thought about it. However, for once, he was at peace staring at the image of his late aunt.

For now.

For now because his appetite had been satisfied. But Jon Albert Murphy knew better than anyone that, at best, this was an extremely fleeting set of circumstances. His insatiable appetite to kill another woman would be back in full force before he could come to terms with it. It always ate away at him long before he was ready to eliminate the source of his anger.

A day lecturer, Murphy was sitting in his cubbyhole of an office—an insult to his honor as far as he was concerned—with the door closed. Even so, the lecturer was carrying on the discussion with the photograph entirely in his head. It wasn't the sort of "conversation" that he could risk having out loud, not when there was a chance that one of his students—or any student, really—could come walking into his office and overhear him.

For the most part, the students who attended Aurora Valley College were a rude bunch of wet-behind-the-ears kids, he thought angrily. Not at all like he had been at their age. He had learned early on, thanks to Aunt Lily, to keep to himself. And to never speak unless he was spoken to—and at times, not even then, because he might find himself the target of someone's unabashed wrath.

But then, the people who frequented the lecture hall where he spoke and the classroom where he taught hadn't been raised by his mother's aunt Lily. Aunt Lily who had used her razor-sharp tongue to create countless bleeding holes in his self-esteem from the very moment she had become his guardian.

Murphy remembered how stunned he had been when he discovered that his white trash mother had decided that she didn't want to be saddled with him any longer. That was when Aunt Lily had stepped up to take over.

At the time, he had been too naïve to understand why Aunt Lily had volunteered to do that. He had just thought that the woman was being kind to him. But he had learned all too quickly that that wasn't the case.

It had been his last innocent thought.

And then, for a moment, the lecturer smiled to himself. Murphy was more than willing to bet that, in the end, Aunt Lily wound up regretting the decision she had made to be his guardian. Things hadn't exactly turned out the way she had planned.

Murphy sighed, resigned, as he looked back at the paper he had half-heartedly been attempting to read.

These so-called "students" who attended Aurora Valley College, they were all a bunch of hopeless illiterates. Sometimes he couldn't help wondering why he bothered wasting his time with them.

But then, he thought, he knew exactly why he was doing this. Not to be dazzled by the magnitude of someone's brain. That was definitely not the reason why he had applied to Aurora Valley College for the position of lecturer in the English Department when it had come up.

He had come to the two-year college for an entirely different reason—a different agenda.

He had come here looking for another sort of gratification. One that Aurora Valley College had been able to provide him with.

Several times over, Murphy recalled with an eerie smile that would have unsettled anyone who looked at it.

Shifting, Murphy tried to make himself comfortable in the hand-me-down office chair he had inherited along with the desk. It was an impossible task as far as he was concerned. Another insult in his eyes.

The chair creaked as he leaned back in it and continued to read the incredibly dull paper. He could almost feel his eyes closing.

Talk about boring, he thought in disgust.

Murphy was surprised that he could read it and somehow still manage to remain awake. It was really a constant battle just to keep his eyes open.

Little by little, he forced himself to shift his mind

to the events he was anticipating happening later on this evening, after classes were over. Later this evening was when he was supposed to get together with Mrs. Lauren Dixon. The vivacious older blonde had asked him for help with her next paper. She had told him that she anticipated problems. Right.

As she made the request, the restaurant waitress had even blushed a little.

Like he didn't even know what was going on.

The corners of his mouth curved as he thought about meeting the woman in some little-frequented, off-campus location. Now all he had to do was decide if tonight was going to be the night when he made his move, or if he was going to put it off until some later date, anticipating the way it would feel.

Sometimes, he told himself, waiting for that final moment was half the fun.

Anticipation, Murphy thought as his pulse sped up and his smile widened, could be everything.

He finished reading the paper he was holding quickly, then decided to award it a giant C plus, far more than the execution was worth in his opinion. Who knew, he might want to cultivate some goodwill with this student at a later date as well.

No stone unturned, he decided with a wicked smile.

Chapter 1

Detective Cheyenne Cavanaugh shifted uncomfortably at her desk and frowned. Up until this point, she had thought that her partner was only talking. Wade did have a tendency to do that. Realizing that he wasn't definitely put a damper on her newly appointed position of police detective. She didn't want to do this without him. It was like attempting to cross the high wire without a net.

"Are you sure about this—really sure?" she asked the man she had been partnered with since she had first walked into the Cold Case Department. Back then, she had not actually been Wade Jessup's partner—she had been more or less his underling. The one who had willingly run his errands in exchange for the privilege of learning from the old-time veteran.

Oh, granted, she could have just as easily learned from one of her siblings or her cousins, or even her uncles. Heaven knew there was no shortage of law enforcement agents milling around at any of the numerous family gatherings that she had attended over the years, or at the actual precinct. But Wade had provided a rather unique take on the job, and to her way of thinking, the more perspectives she was exposed to, the larger her field of learning became. She was like the proverbial thirsty sponge, soaking it all up as quickly as she was exposed to it.

The corners of Wade's mouth curved spasmodically as he looked at her.

"Yes, I'm sure," he answered in that raspy voice she had come to instantly recognize and gravitate toward. "I'm sorry, kid, but it's already a done deal," he told her. "The furniture is all in the moving van and I've packed all my bags. Actually," the man corrected himself, "Beth was the one who packed my bags." He laughed under his breath. "She said if she left it up to me to do, it would take another six months, if not longer, and she's just chomping at the bit to get going." Wade smiled kindly as he looked at his young partner. "Don't forget, Arkansas is home to her."

"But it's not home to you, Wade," Cheyenne insisted, pointing the fact out sullenly.

Wade's thin shoulders rose and then fell in a careless shrug. "So I'll adjust. Don't forget, I adjusted to you, didn't I, kid?" he asked her with a laugh, trying to bring her around as he made his point.

Her eyes met Wade's. "Hell, Wade, I was easy to adjust to," she told her partner defensively.

"Ha! You think so, huh?" Wade remarked with a laugh. And then his expression softened just a little as he looked at her. "Don't worry, kid. You'll adjust to your new partner, whoever he or she might be, in no time flat," Wade told her. "I guarantee it."

Cheyenne sighed, far from won over. "Damn it, Wade, I barely adjusted to you," she remembered aloud, recalling the early days of their partnership. And then she looked at him, attempting to appeal to the older man's sense of fair play. "Are you sure you can't talk your wife into staying?"

Wade eyed Cheyenne incredulously as he laughed at Cheyenne's suggestion under his breath. "Hell, kid, you've met Beth. Did she strike you as someone who could be talked into *anything* she didn't want to be talked into?" he asked the young woman he had referred to—more than once—as the best partner he had ever had.

Cheyenne did not answer his question, or at least she did not answer it directly. Instead, she made a request. "Let me have a crack at her, Wade."

"Not on your life," he told her with a laugh. "I know what you can be like and I want to go on living a little longer once I transfer to that precinct in Arkansas," he told Cheyenne. Slipping his arm around Cheyenne's shoulders, he gave her a quick, friendly hug. "It'll be all right," he promised her.

Cheyenne raised her chin as if she took his words

to be a challenge. "And if it's not?" she asked. "Then what?"

Wade laughed that raspy laugh of his that she was going to miss sorely. "You'll box their ears," he declared knowingly. "And don't worry, my money's on you, kid."

Cheyenne frowned. Deeply. Her slender eyebrows knitted together, forming a straight line. "I really wish that I had your confidence," she informed her about-to-be-former partner.

"That's because you're also not conceited, which is something you've always had to your credit," he pointed out confidently. And then he told her with a wide smile, "Anyone who gets partnered with you is going to be a damn lucky person, kid. Trust me on that."

"As I remember it, that wasn't the way you saw it when you initially found out that that the chief of d's was making me your new partner."

"Initially," Wade conceded with a nod of his head. "But what I was actually attempting to do was keep you on your toes." Wade's brown eyes met hers as he confided, "There's nothing more off-putting than working with someone who has a huge ego the size of a giant pizza."

"I didn't have a huge ego," Cheyenne protested.

A smile graced his lips as Wade shrugged his shoulders. "If you say so, kid," he told her cavalierly. And then his expression softened a little as he looked at her. "You're Cheyenne Cavanaugh," he reminded the young woman. "You can—and will—get through this."

"*Detective* Cheyenne Cavanaugh," she corrected him. The title still felt very new to her and she loved the sound of it and that the word *detective* rolled off her tongue as easily as it did. Lord knew it took a great deal of studying for her to earn the title.

"See?" Wade asked as he picked up the briefcase he had just finished stuffing with all his remaining miscellaneous papers. He smiled at Cheyenne. "It's just as I predicted. You're getting through it already."

She knew she could, but it would definitely take her a while. It was not about to happen in a blink of an eye. "I'd get through it better if you stayed," she said in all seriousness.

Wade patted his partner's shoulder. There was compassion in his eyes. He knew that change wasn't easy for some and Cheyenne numbered among those.

"I would if I could, Cheyenne, but I can't." He smiled at her. "You'll do fine, kid. My money's on you. It always has been," he told her with no shortage of confidence. And then he looked at his watch. It was time for him to wrap this all up or contrary to what he had said, he might never leave. "Well, I've got to go, Cheyenne. Beth's picking me up and she hates it when I'm late."

Cheyenne had a sudden thought. "Could Beth come up here to come get you? I'd like to say good-bye to her as well," Cheyenne told him, getting somewhat creative when it came to making excuses for him not to leave.

The expression on Wade's face told his former partner that he saw right through her. Not bothering with a somber expression, Wade laughed out loud at the suggestion that Cheyenne had just given him. The look he gave her all but asked if she actually thought that was going to work.

"Oh no, I'm not about to ask Beth to come up here. Senility has not set in yet," Wade told her. And then he paused beside her and like a doting uncle her gave her cheek a very quick kiss. "Take care of yourself, kid," he told her. His expression softened as he looked into her face. "You really were a great partner." He gave her arm a quick squeeze. "I'll send you my address and you can send me a line or two about how things are going whenever you have some free time and get the chance."

Her eyes narrowed a little as she pinned Wade with a look. "I can also send you the riot act as well."

Wade laughed as he gave her quick two-finger salute. His expression seemed to say, *Always the fighter.*

"I bet you can, too," the man acknowledged. And then he glanced at his watch again. "I've really got to get going," he told her. "Stay safe, kid," the man added as he began to take his leave.

"I'd stay safer if you continued being my partner," Cheyenne called after him in all seriousness.

For the most part, she was an independent person, but Wade had made an impression on her and she realized that, although it embarrassed her to admit it even to herself, she had grown attached to him.

Wade raised his hand above his head as he waved goodbye to her. Cutting the conversation short, he kept on walking. He was acutely aware of the fact that when it came to Cheyenne, one word would just continue to lead to another—and another. What he needed to do was stop talking and keep walking or he would never leave.

So he did.

Cheyenne pressed her lips together. She knew this was ridiculous, but she missed the man already. He had been a good, decent partner and he hadn't been out to get anything from her or from her connection to the rest of the Cavanaughs. He was just interested in being a good detective and turning her into one as well.

And for her part, Cheyenne had been determined to learn from him, not interested in taking advantage of the fact that when it came to the police department, she uniquely belonged to an almost dynasty-like group of people.

Cheyenne sighed as she looked at the file she was reviewing. That protracted goodbye with her former partner had happened almost four days ago.

Funny how that felt like an eternity.

She had technically been on her own for four days now. She was exceedingly aware of the fact that Brian Cavanaugh, the chief of detectives as well as her uncle, was actively looking to pair her with another partner. But for her part, she was in no hurry for that to happen. The other side of being paired off was preparing herself for the inevitable loss.

She had already gone through that. In the past six months, she had had the man she had assumed she would wind up marrying just abandon her because she wasn't willing to pull up her roots, leave her beloved extensive family and move to the East Coast. That was what Steve, her ex-fiancé, had wanted—and expected from a soon-to-be wife. And now her partner, a man who had trained her and carefully taught her how to be the kind of detective she felt she was meant to be, had left her as well.

She definitely wasn't looking to join forces with anyone else only to have that sort of thing happen to her again. Or at least certainly not any time soon.

So instead of ruminating over it, she threw herself headlong into her work with gusto.

There was no shortage of cold cases for her to dive into. She just needed to pick ones that sparked her sleuthing heart, cases that cried out for her special set of skills.

To remain on the safe side, Cheyenne didn't just pick one cold case—she picked several. She felt rather certain that if she applied herself to a number of cases, she was bound to be able to make some sort of headway on at least one of them, if not more.

The way she tackled her work was to come in early, stay late and work almost around the clock on the cases on her desk until she felt that she couldn't keep her eyes open for a second longer.

Cheyenne sighed and sat back in her chair. She closed her eyes for a moment in order to try to keep them from aching.

Taking another deep breath, she formed a pyramid with her fingertips directly above her nose.

Go home, Chey. You're not doing anyone any good this way. You can get a fresh start in the morning.

But her pep talk, as well intentioned as it was, did not help. She remained sitting at her desk, the file on Rita Connor's murder lying open in front of her. The words in the file were almost taunting her.

She stared at them, rereading the words until they all but swam in front of her. It didn't help. Enlightenment did not come. Her thoughts about the crime had no rhyme or reason to them. Cheyenne was aware of the fact that some murders occurred for no reason and those were much more difficult to solve.

It was almost as if the killer was standing somewhere hidden nearby taunting her.

She looked at the time of death marked in the file. There was actually a question mark in it. The killer could very well have committed the murder recently. The ME hadn't been able to pinpoint the time of death because the body had been discovered floating in an abandoned pool that in turn belonged to an abandoned house. It had been concluded that the victim, an older blonde who appeared to have been very mindful of keeping up on her looks, had died in the pool. A great deal of water was found in her lungs.

Due to the marks on her throat, it appeared as if the killer had strangled her and held her underwater until she had drowned.

Had the killer planned all this out carefully, or was this just a murder of opportunity?

"Why did you have to leave now, Wade? We could have solved this murder together and you could have gone out with a bang, " Cheyenne murmured under her breath.

She glanced at the phone on her desk, fighting the temptation to pick up the receiver and call her former partner. She knew that this was the sort of crime he loved poring over. Cheyenne debated using the number Wade had given her.

"And say what?" Cheyenne challenged herself, continuing to murmur under her breath. "That you can't solve the very first murder that comes across your desk now that your partner is gone? Since when have you become so helpless?" she asked herself in a wave of disgust.

She noticed one of the detectives, Abe Hamilton, looking her way and realized that she needed to keep her voice down—or better yet, not say anything out loud at all.

Cheyenne flashed a smile at Abe, then cleared her throat, as if something had impeded her breathing and she was most definitely not talking to herself.

"I'm fighting a cold," she told the detective, who was staring at her curiously.

After a beat Abe nodded as if what she had said made perfect sense to him. "So tell me, what are you taking for it?"

"I don't know, what will you give me for it?" Cheyenne asked before she could stop herself.

"Well, that cold of yours you're talking about has clearly gone to your head," her uncle Brian commented, amused as he walked into the room. "Would you like to go home?"

"No, sir. What I want to do is solve this crime— sooner rather than later," Cheyenne added with feeling.

Brian nodded, satisfied with her response and with the fact that she really didn't seem to be ill.

"Good answer," he told her. "By the way, there's someone here who I'd like you to meet, Cheyenne." The chief of d's turned toward the doorway, beckoning to the man who was standing off in the distance, talking to someone else.

Cheyenne's stomach sank even before she turned around. She had a feeling that the chief of d's was about to introduce her to her future partner.

And she really didn't want to meet him yet.

Chapter 2

Cheyenne knew it was a given rule that no one worked solo in the police force. At least not for long. Partnerships were encouraged.

There were of course unavoidable situations in the various departments where detectives went solo, but none of these situations lasted for more than a few days. So when she turned around to face whoever the chief of d's had brought with him, Cheyenne braced herself—at the same time mentally upbraiding Wade for having left Aurora and abandoning her.

Never mind that he had done it for the sake of his marriage and to ultimately please his wife. The bottom line was that Wade had left their day-to-day existence and a rather successful partnership. She was on her own.

Well, at least her uncle looked rather satisfied with the way things had turned out, and for the most part, Brian Cavanaugh was a decent man who always kept his eye on his people, determined to do his best for them and by them. He had not been wrong yet, Cheyenne thought, but then, there was always a first time.

Cheyenne had really no idea what to expect. But whatever it was, she was not expecting that her new partner was going to be an exceptionally good-looking man with dark hair and a smile that could melt the beholder from a distance of approximately fifty feet—if not a bit more.

She took in a deep breath after she realized that she had stopped breathing altogether.

This was not good.

Belatedly Cheyenne took in another breath as she waited for her pulse to slow down and her heart to resume beating normally. It took her longer than she was happy about. Having this sort of reaction was just not like her.

Rather than her uncle making the initial introduction to her new partner, Cheyenne heard a deep male voice say, "Hi, I'm Jefferson McDougall. You can call me Jeff or McDougall or 'hey you' or just about anything in between you feel comfortable with," the six-foot-two detective told her as he leaned forward and took her hand, shaking it.

It took Cheyenne a moment to respond. Caught somewhat off guard, she allowed the new man to continue holding her hand and shaking it. After another moment, she ended the connection.

"We'll work on it," Cheyenne responded noncommittally to her choice regarding what to call him. She took a step back.

Rather than take offense, or think she was being unfriendly, Jefferson smiled at her. "That sounds good to me."

The chief of d's was standing off to the side, watching the initial interaction between the two brand-new partners. Brian nodded to himself, satisfied. He had made a good call, he thought, pairing his niece with this Texas transplant.

"All right, McDougall, let me introduce you to your lieutenant. Earl Holloway," the chief of d's told Cheyenne's new partner.

Brian placed his hand on the new detective's shoulder as he turned the young man around. He directed him toward the back of the room and the glass-encased office that was located there.

The chief of d's looked over his shoulder at Cheyenne, who had remained where she was, rooted to the spot at her desk. His niece looked as if she didn't know whether or not she was supposed to tag along. Had this been Wade, there would have been no question in her mind.

Brian gave her a little verbal push. "Would you like to come with us, Detective, seeing as how you two are going to be a working duo for the foreseeable future?" the chief of d's asked his niece.

Cheyenne rose from her desk. "At least for the time being," she told her uncle, feeling it prudent to add in that particular proviso.

Brian didn't bother keeping his wide smile to himself. As a rule, he enjoyed his work and smiled easily, especially when things were going well. Solving crimes was in his blood. So was working with the people who solved them. And a good detective was a good detective. It made no difference to him if he was related to them or not.

"Oh, I think it'll be longer than that," he told his niece. He was aware that Cheyenne didn't like change and hadn't been happy when her partner had announced that he was leaving, but the chief of d's was fairly confident that this would turn out to be the right sort of change for the newly minted detective.

Cheyenne took a breath. She was doing her best to reassure herself that it was all going to turn out all right no matter what.

She could tell that her new partner was looking at her but at the same time she was managing to avoid making any actual eye contact as she secretly regarded him. She couldn't help wondering what she was ultimately going to wind up getting herself into by going along with this new partner being assigned to her.

She walked quickly, staying abreast of her uncle and deliberately stepping ahead of this new partner she had been paired up with.

For his part McDougall was happy to just hang

back, allowing Cheyenne to make her way ahead of him. It wasn't just chivalry that dictated his actions, although that was the largest part of it. It was also the view that being in this particular position afforded him. The woman had to have, he quickly concluded, pretty much the perfect figure.

Jefferson was not about to deny the fact that he liked the view he was looking at.

He liked it a great deal.

What still remained to be seen was if this new partner of his had a personality that matched her sterling figure. He hadn't asked around about Cheyenne Cavanaugh when he had found out that he was being partnered with the woman because, first of all, he doubted that he would get a totally honest answer since this woman belonged to the first family of law enforcement in the city of Aurora. And secondly, he liked forming his own opinion when it came to matters like this. He didn't particularly care to take anyone else's word for something—he needed to decide on his own.

Admittedly, the first thing that had struck him when he saw her siting here in the Cold Case Department was that the woman was incredibly easy on the eyes. That wasn't the most important thing and he knew that, but it certainly didn't hurt matters any. Not by a long shot.

Working with the woman on an everyday basis, Jefferson thought, should certainly prove to be exceedingly interesting.

Thinking about that, Jefferson was still smiling to himself as he crossed the threshold and walked into the lieutenant's office behind his new partner and the chief of d's.

Lieutenant Earl Holloway was a middle-aged man with a very full head of salt-and-pepper hair. Since even before he had joined the police force, Holloway had firmly believed in staying in fighting shape. Consequently the man looked younger than his actual age despite the fact that his hair had begun turning gray six months before he had turned thirty-five.

The lieutenant half rose in his chair now, greeting the three people who came into his office. The man gestured toward the three seats that had been arranged in front of his desk.

"Sit, please," Holloway requested, his deep brown eyes sweeping over the three individuals who had filed into his small office. Two, of course, he knew from frequently interacting with them. The third had come to his attention late last night when the Texas transplant had arrived in the Cold Case Department, saying that he had been sent here on the recommendation of Shane Cavanaugh, the head of the CSI Department. Oddly enough, Lieutenant Holloway had been told, the two had run into one another in Texas while McDougall was rethinking his choices and the direction that his career was taking.

"So, I hear that you went into law enforcement straight out of your stint with the Marines," the lieutenant said. Holloway smiled knowingly at Jefferson. "I guess that actually gives us something in common, Detective McDougall."

"How so, sir?" Jefferson asked politely, although he had a feeling that he already knew the answer to that. Still, he thought it only polite to ask the man.

The lieutenant smiled. There was nothing he enjoyed more than reliving his glory days as a Marine. He felt as if his years as a Marine testified to how courageous he had been as a young man—he had managed to fight overseas and return to the States without getting so much as a single scratch on his body.

"I was a Marine too," Lieutenant Holloway answered. And then he waved away his own words with his hand. "But this meeting isn't about me, McDougall. It's about you and, of course, your new partner, Detective Cheyenne Cavanaugh," he said. The lieutenant nodded his head toward Cheyenne. "Detective Cavanaugh here recently lost her partner."

Jefferson turned toward the two people sitting to his right. "I'm very sorry to hear that," he told his new partner with sincerity. "If you don't mind my asking, Detective, what happened?"

Cheyenne's expression hardened ever so slightly at the question. She didn't know if this new man was being sincere or just playing dumb. She decided to answer her new partner's question before her uncle had the chance to respond, thus clearing the matter up. "He moved to Arkansas so he and his wife could be near her family."

Jefferson was surprised at the answer. He had thought that this new partner's previous partner had either died or been seriously hurt. Embarrassed over his mistake, the man backtracked.

"That's a shame," Jefferson conceded. "I heard that he was a good man." That much was true. He noticed that his new partner's expression brightened ever so slightly. "But his loss is definitely my gain," Jefferson declared with a nod of his head.

Cheyenne's eyes narrowed just a little. He was playing her, she thought. Well, her guard was not about to go down. "Isn't your assessment of the situation just a little premature?" she asked the ex-Marine. "You don't even know me yet."

Rather than look embarrassed over her challenge, Jefferson smiled. "I guess you can call it a gut feeling."

A couple of her uncles as well as several of her cousins were quite big on trusting their gut feelings. She wasn't about to credit this newcomer with being correct in trusting his just yet. Not at this point.

"I'd say as far as you're concerned, it was more of a shot in the dark than anything else," Cheyenne informed her new partner coldly.

Jefferson did not seem to take any offense. "I guess we'll just have to see about that," her new partner told her cheerfully.

Blocking out the other two men seated in the small glass office, she fixed Jefferson with a penetrating look that was meant to pin him to his chair. "I guess we will," she answered the man stoically.

Looking to avoid any argument in the making, Holloway said to the newest detective joining his group, "The chief of d's gave me your file. At this point, I only gave it a cursory glance, but I did take note of the fact that you have a rather impressive record with the El Paso Police Department." Holloway flashed a wide smile at Jefferson. "Hope that comes with a boatload of patience as well because you're really going to need it when it comes to dealing with cold cases."

The lieutenant wasn't telling him anything new, McDougall thought. "In my experience, most crimes don't get solved in a hurry, sir," Jefferson replied.

The lieutenant nodded with a smile. "That's been my experience as well," Holloway agreed. "If you don't mind my asking, why did you leave the Marines?"

It wasn't the question that the detective had been expecting. He would have expected one along the lines of asking him about his police experience. "I just felt that my time was up, sir," the detective answered. "And that I could do more good as a police officer than as a Marine working my way up. I worked in the El Paso office to orient myself then decided I might be happier stationed in a California office. When I asked around, I heard nothing but very good things about the Aurora Police Department, so I thought that since I was packing up, I should make the most of it."

"And here you are," Holloway concluded with a smile.

"Lucky us," Cheyenne murmured under her breath.

She had yet to decide whether or not the new detective was on the level.

"Something you'd like to share, Detective?" Holloway asked, looking pointedly at Cheyenne.

"Not a thing, sir," Cheyenne answered without blinking an eye. The remark had just slipped out before she could stop it.

The lieutenant scanned the small room. "Anyone else have anything to say?" Holloway asked, then looked up at the chief of d's. "Chief?"

"Yes," Brian replied. He looked at the two detectives he had ushered into the lieutenant's office. "Let's get to work, shall we?"

Knowing that this signaled an end to the impromptu meeting, Cheyenne and her new partner rose to their feet almost in unison.

Jefferson took the lead and waved for her to walk out of the room first. Cheyenne said nothing as she moved out in front of the transplanted Texan.

Brian followed the new partners, closing the office door behind him.

There were only a few steps back into the main office and a few more to Cheyenne's desk.

Jefferson looked around the area, just slightly disoriented.

"Where would you like me to sit?" he asked, tossing the question out to both his new partner and the chief of d's.

Cheyenne bit back the urge to answer *Texas* in response to the man's question just as the chief of d's responded to her new partner by saying, "Right there looks about right."

"Right there" turned out to be a location that did not please Cheyenne. It was the desk positioned right next to hers.

"That's Wade's desk," she protested with a deep frown without thinking.

"That *was* Wade's desk," Brian corrected his niece. "From what I hear, unless you know something that I don't, he's not going to be using it anymore, which means that it's going to be empty and McDougall here will be free to use it. Right, Detective?" Brian asked, looking directly at her.

Cheyenne repressed a sigh and pressed her lips together to keep back any unwanted comments. "Right, Chief."

Brian smiled. "Glad you agree." He turned his attention toward the new man. "The detective here will show you how we do things around here, McDougall," he told the recently transferred detective. "And if you have any questions about anything—anything at all," Brian emphasized, "my door is always open."

And with that, Brian Cavanaugh patted the new man on the shoulder and then walked out of the Cold Case Department, leaving the new duo to begin fermenting their partnership.

Chapter 3

What Cheyenne really wanted to do was distance herself from this person who had unexpectedly invaded her life as her partner. Instead, she just decided to throw herself into going through the old case files the way she had been doing since she had first transferred into this department.

But she also knew that wouldn't be right, nor was it what the chief of d's or Lieutenant Holloway would expect her to do with this new person who had joined her work group.

They all worked as a team, not just here but in all the different departments that made up the entire police force. It was a given. Moreover, she was a Cavanaugh, which meant that she had a larger stake in the police force than the usual police officer or detective did. She had to work harder at the job and put in longer hours whenever necessary, and she had been raised to do so willingly.

It was actually this attachment to the police department that was the very reason why she hadn't agreed to transfer to the East Coast when her ex-fiancé had tried to convince her to move there with him.

What her mindset meant in this particular case was that she knew that it was up to her to take the initial steps to introduce her new partner to the other people who were working within the Cold Case Department.

Cheyenne didn't mind being friendly, but she wasn't thrilled about being forced into this position, either. Still, a responsibility was a responsibility. She had to face up to it and do whatever was required of her. She had never so much as been accused of being unfriendly before. But right now, missing Wade, her original partner, was getting in the way of living up to that.

Cheyenne raised her chin, silently telling herself that she couldn't allow that to ruin her reputation as a team player. She could focus on what she was feeling tonight, after she got back to her house. Right now, she needed to show Jefferson around and introduce the man to the people he would be working with.

"You need to meet some of the people in the office," she told Jefferson, stopping short of sitting down at her desk.

That, in turn, prevented the detective from taking his own seat.

Jefferson looked at his new partner in surprise. He had to admit that he hadn't expected her to go out of her way like this. That he would have expected this from the chief of d's, absolutely. Chief Brian Cavanaugh came across like the personification of friendliness. But as far as Cheyenne Cavanaugh went, although the woman was exceptionally attractive, she looked rather dour and not all that friendly when he observed her.

But then, maybe he had misjudged the woman, the detective thought. And this was unusual for him. He wasn't usually quick to jump to a conclusion.

He needed to rein himself in, he thought. That would be better for them both.

"Agreed," Jefferson replied amiably, curious to see just where this would wind up going.

"All right, so let's get to it," Cheyenne said.

She had almost slipped and said, *Let's get this over with*, but had managed to stop herself at the very last minute.

Instead, she moved away from her desk and made her way over to the two nearby detectives whose desks were butted up against one another.

"Guys, I'd like you to meet Detective Jefferson McDougall. He's freshly transplanted from the El Paso, Texas, police department. He's going to be taking Wade's place now that my former partner decided that he wanted to move to Arkansas." She tactfully did not add what she thought of that move.

Cheyenne only half turned toward her new partner as she waved a hand at first one detective and then the other as she made her introductions.

"This is Detective Jose Gonzales and Detective Jordan Nguyen," she told Jefferson, then smiled. "Between the two of them, Gonzales and Nguyen have twenty-eight and a half years' worth of knowledge and experience."

Jose was the first one on his feet, a heartbeat behind Jordan. Jose grinned broadly as he extended his wide, beefy hand toward Cheyenne's new partner. Grasping the man's hand, Jose shook it firmly.

"She likes to exaggerate whenever she can," the older man told Jefferson as he nodded toward Cheyenne.

"But not by much," Jordan added seriously, shaking the new detective's hand next. "If you've got any questions, feel free to ask them. If we can't answer them—"

"They'll make something up," Cheyenne couldn't resist telling her new partner.

Jose pretended to frown at Cheyenne's comment as he shook his head. "That's what's wrong with this younger generation," he told his partner, Jordan. "No respect for their elders."

Cheyenne fluttered her lashes at the slightly stocky older detective. "Respect has to be earned, Detective Gonzales," she told the man, doing her best to look serious as she said it.

Gonzales laughed shortly. "I don't envy you, McDougall, being paired up with this one." He jerked his thumb in Cheyenne's direction. "Listen, if it gets to be too much for you, I know a good bar that's located not too far from here. The place is run by former police officers and detectives. They'll make you feel right at home in minutes."

Cheyenne turned toward the older detective. "Are you saying I'm going to drive my new partner to drink?" she asked the man pointedly.

Gonzales held his hands up as if to protest his innocence. "That was never my intention," he told Cheyenne. "I'm sure he's perfectly capable of making up his own mind about what you have to offer. I just wanted him to know that there were a number of possible solutions available to him if it gets to be too much for him."

"Your partner's new," Nguyen explained his own partner's thinking to Cheyenne. "Right now, he doesn't know about our popular hangout."

Cheyenne had a hunch where this was going. "When the time comes, I'm sure that you'll take him there. All I ask is that you let McDougall get one sober day in under his belt before you introduce him to our friendly corner bar."

Nguyen nodded. "You survive one day with Cheyenne here and we will personally take you there to celebrate," he promised. "As for today, welcome to the Cold Case Department."

The corners of Jefferson's mouth curved as he nodded at the two detectives, returning their greetings. "Thanks, guys."

Cheyenne placed her hand squarely on her new partner's back, ushering the man over toward other detectives and officers who were in the room, men and women who he needed to get to know, at least in a cursory manner.

"You still have other people to meet," she told Jefferson. "You'll find that they each have their own special field of expertise and that their knowledge might come in handy when you least expect it. To solve these old crimes, we're going to need to cover a great deal more ground."

Jefferson eyed her thoughtfully. "Are you planning on making these introductions all in one day?" he asked.

"And if I am?" she asked him, giving him no indication which way she intended to lean. "Would you have a problem with that?"

Jefferson shook his head. "No, ma'am," he answered.

About to lead her new partner toward another area in the room, Cheyenne stopped short and held her hand up, calling for a halt.

She turned toward him, far from happy. "'Ma'am'?" she repeated, looking at him in disbelief. "Do I look like a 'ma'am' to you?" she asked him, stunned.

"I'm from Texas," Jefferson told the detective. "Addressing a woman as 'ma'am' is a sign of respect."

Cheyenne's eyes narrowed as she took exception to his explanation. "It's ageism," she informed the new detective. "I'm not your mother or your maiden aunt. I am your partner. You can call me 'Cavanaugh,' or 'Detective' or 'partner' or even, if we're working particularly late and you're punchy, 'Cheyenne.' But if you call me 'ma'am' again, I'll rip your tongue out and use it as a bookmark. Do I make myself clear, McDougall?" she asked her new partner.

"Perfectly," he answered without a moment's hesitation. In addition he had the good grace not to grin at her words.

Cheyenne inclined her head, nodding her approval. "Good. I have a few more people for you to meet," she told him, beckoning for the detective to follow her, which he did. Rather quickly at that.

The first of the people she brought her partner over to meet was Detective Barbara Baker, who had, according to Cheyenne, been part of the department ever since it had been first formed. Before then, Baker had been part of the Missing Persons Department Her crossover knowledge was rather extensive.

"She has an incredible amount of patience as well," Cheyenne told him, thinking that Baker might have actually been better suited to work with McDougall than she was. But that would mean that she might have to work with Baker's partner, Kevin Calhoun, and she had quickly learned that Detective Calhoun liked to take the easy way out whenever he could—which unfortunately for him was not as often as he would have liked. But that, Cheyenne reminded herself, was not her problem.

Bringing Jefferson over to the two desks, Cheyenne dutifully introduced her new partner to Baker and Calhoun. She noticed that McDougall seemed to take to this pair like he had to the first two detectives who she had introduced him to. The man was exceedingly friendly.

It seemed, Cheyenne thought as the introduction process continued throughout the day, that there wasn't anyone that her new partner didn't interact with well, and no one he seemed to have any difficulties with. The man could have gotten along with the devil himself, she concluded.

By the end of the day, Cheyenne had managed to introduce him to everyone she felt he might find helpful with any investigation he was involved in. Except for, of course, Valri, their resident computer wizard. But that, Cheyenne promised, would be an introduction for another time, when the need came up.

"Tomorrow," Cheyenne told her new partner at the end of the day, "the real work will begin. Slowly," she emphasized, hoping that the detective was as long on patience as she thought he was. "But it will begin."

"What are you working on?" Jefferson asked as they began packing up for the day. "I'm assuming that we're going to be working a case together." There was a hopeful note in the detective's voice.

Cheyenne had been working on several cases concurrently, looking for similarities between the cases or something that might wind up triggering something for her and tying the cold cases together. So far, though, she had come up empty. But she felt, that she might be missing something or overlooking it. Something of vital importance.

Maybe if she talked it out, it would become clearer to her in the morning. That was something to hope for, Cheyenne told herself.

"I'll lay it out for you in the morning," she promised, referring to what she was working on. "Right now, you have put in a full day of orientation and your brain probably needs a time-out to rest."

But her partner protested at being sent off like this. This was just the first day and he wanted to absorb as much as he could. "I'm used to long hours."

"And you'll get them, I promise," she told him, adding, "far more than you bargained for. But this is your first day here and the chief of d's doesn't want to have you run out screaming until you have at least a second day under your belt." She grinned at her new partner. "We try not to overwhelm you too fast."

"You're exaggerating," Jefferson laughed indulgently at his partner's words.

Cheyenne gave him a look that had been known stop other men dead in their tracks because they weren't sure just how to read it. "Am I?" she challenged.

"You know, it's going to take me some time, but I fully intend to figure out when you're kidding and when you're serious," he told her.

Cheyenne flashed a knowing look in her new partner's direction. She didn't intend to become anyone's flash card and she certainly wasn't about to become that easy to read. "Well, good luck with that," she told him.

"Are you daring me?" Jefferson asked, raising a quizzical eyebrow in her direction.

"No, just wishing you luck," she told him with an innocent expression.

"Don't torture him too much or he won't come back tomorrow, Cavanaugh," Gonzales told her as he took his jacket off the hook. The detective slipped it on, getting ready to leave the precinct.

"Oh, don't worry. He'll be back," Cheyenne said knowingly, her eyes meeting her partner's. "The man likes a challenge. Don't you, McDougall?"

"My dad told me that all of life is a challenge," Jefferson told her as they walked out of the office and to the elevator together.

Cheyenne's mouth quirked in a quick smile as she considered the relationship Jefferson might have shared with his father back in the day. As of yet, she really didn't know that much about her partner, or any of his family.

"Sounds like your dad's a smart man," she commented.

A distant, wistful look passed over Jefferson's face before he answered, "He was."

Cheyenne read between the lines. "Then he's gone?" she asked quietly, her heart going out to her partner.

Jefferson nodded. "Five years ago," he told her.

For a moment, pity came into Cheyenne's eyes. "I'm sorry to hear that."

Jefferson raised and lowered his shoulders, dismissing the element of sorrow that was ordinarily tied to death. He wasn't looking for pity, nor did he want any. "He died doing what he liked," Jefferson told her. "That's all any of us can ask for."

Cheyenne pressed her lips together. Well, this didn't happen often. Perhaps, on this rare occasion, she had made an initial wrong call. Could it be that she and her new partner were going to get along after all?

At least she could hope, Cheyenne thought.

When the elevator arrived, they got on and took it down to the ground floor. Within two minutes, it opened again and they got off.

"See you tomorrow," Jefferson told her, stepping back so that she could get off first.

"Tomorrow," Cheyenne echoed, then stopped short. Turning toward her partner, she surprised herself by asking, "Would you like to stop off at the local watering hole?"

Way to go, Chey. Talk about not keeping your distance.

Chapter 4

Taking a few quick steps, Jefferson caught up with his new partner.

"You mean with you?" he asked.

Cheyenne smirked at her partner as if he had just asked her a really dumb question. "No, with some homeless person looking for someone to buy him a drink. Yes, of course with me," she answered him, then decided that maybe she had spoken too hastily and, at least at this point of their association, she should really qualify the responses she gave the detective. "Unless you'd rather not share a drink with me. I don't want you to feel like I'm holding your back up against a wall and making you do this."

"No, you're not forcing me to do anything. I'd really like to have a drink with you. I'd think of it as toasting our new partnership. But I don't really know my way around Aurora yet," he confessed. "You're going to have to show me where this popular local hangout is located."

"No problem," Cheyenne assured him. "I can definitely lead the way for you to get over there. Just keep my vehicle in your sights and follow it there. Just promise me that once you get there and get a drink, you won't wind up overimbibing."

"On my first day?" he asked, looking at her incredulously. "No way I would ever do that. Actually, I wouldn't do that on my twentieth day—or twentieth year," he added. "As a law enforcement officer, I have a certain responsibility to remain on my best behavior. That means if I intend to overindulge, I don't go out. Or, at the very least, I don't drive anywhere and just hire a cab. That wouldn't be setting a good example for anyone, not the people I work with and not the townspeople I work for."

"'Townspeople'?" she questioned, doing her best to hide her amusement at his terminology.

Jefferson didn't see why the word he had used had tickled her to this extent. "Yes, townspeople," he repeated, then clarified, "The people who live in the town."

Cheyenne laughed softly under her breath. "I have a three-year-old nephew who would be pointing at you right now and saying 'he talks funny,'" she told Jefferson.

Her partner looked unfazed. "Townspeople," he repeated. "That's the way they talk where I come from."

She nodded, leading the way over to her vehicle. "I kind of figured that," she said. Pausing next to her car, Cheyenne dictated the address of the bar so he had some idea of where he was driving when he followed her. "It's not too far from here. And I'll be sure to drive slowly so I don't wind up losing you."

"You won't lose me," her partner told her with unshakeable confidence.

Cheyenne turned to look at McDougall and shook her head. "You know, you're really going to have to do something about that inferiority complex of yours," she told her partner.

The grin that Jefferson flashed her was wide and for a moment actually succeeded in pulling her in, before she was able to successfully block both the smile and the effect it was having on her. "I'm working on it," he told her.

Cheyenne raised a skeptical eyebrow as she looked at her partner. "Well, work harder," she said.

"It's at the top of my list of things to do," McDougall told her, opening his car door and getting in. The detective started up his vehicle, preparing to follow hers out of the parking lot.

As she drove, Cheyenne kept one eye on her rearview mirror, making sure that she didn't lose sight of her new partner's vehicle. The last thing she wanted to do was lose the man on the way to the bar.

Traffic at this hour was rather slow, but considering how close the establishment was to the police station, it hardly took any time at all to get there. In addition, for once she wasn't really in any hurry to get to the establishment where people from the police force gathered at the end of their workday. Cheyenne's primary goal in going to the bar was to be the first one to bring her new partner there and to introduce him around to the people from the force who frequented the place. She thought it might make him feel more welcomed to the force.

After she did her part, she would go, leaving the former Marine on his own. She had a feeling that the transplanted Texas detective would do rather well here. The bar was a friendly place and from what she had already assessed, McDougall was friendly as well. Friendly and outgoing. Those traits would do him very well in his choice of careers.

The small parking lot behind the short, squat building that housed the bar was almost full. She pulled up into one of the few spaces that were still available. The detective she had brought here took one of the others at the other end of the lot. Cheyenne got out of her vehicle and waited for her partner to join her.

"This isn't much of a parking lot," Jefferson commented as he crossed over to her. "Do they do much business here?" he asked.

"They do. You would be surprised at how much business transpires here. This place has three partners at this point. Latecomers usually wind up parking across the street, somewhere up or down the block. Farther if necessary," she added. "But proximity and walking distance aren't the main draw when it comes to the bar. Talking to your fellow law enforcement officers is." She paused for a moment, wanting to frame what she was about to say next. "Now, I really don't think you're going to need any help in this matter. All I'm going to do is provide initial introductions and I'm sure that you can take it from there."

They were now at the entrance of the bar, an unpretentious, welcoming little building. Jefferson opened the door and held it for his new partner. "You're being extremely helpful here, Cheyenne," he told her. "And I really appreciate it."

She walked into the bar ahead of him. "Hey, helpful is my middle name," she told him with a laugh. "Besides, it's up to me to provide you with the tools you're going to need to do this job right."

Jefferson raised a quizzical eyebrow. "You consider a mug of beer a tool?" he asked Cheyenne, intrigued with her reasoning.

Her mouth curved in amusement. "Sometimes."

Hearing that, the detective laughed to himself, getting a kick out of his partner's comment. "That's one I'm going to have to remember."

"Feel free to claim that as your own," she told him, and then she grew serious. "Like I told you earlier, we're a team here in the Cold Case Department. You never know when one tiny clue, one little tidbit, might wind up helping us solve the case."

The man behind the bar, Martin Colbert, a former

police detective who had been in several different departments during his career before he retired after putting in almost thirty years, looked Cheyenne's way and nodded a greeting at her.

Cheyenne waved at the heavyset man. "Hi, Marty, I brought my new partner in to meet you."

Setting aside the cloth he was using to clean the counter—which didn't look as if it needed any actual cleaning—the man put out his hand toward Jefferson. "Hello, New Partner." He cocked his head, looking at him with curiosity. "You got a name?"

Jefferson didn't hesitate in taking the extended hand. "As a matter of fact, I do. It's McDougall. Jefferson McDougall," he said, introducing himself formally.

"Nice to meet you, Jefferson McDougall." Marty released Jefferson's hand and cocked his head, listening more closely. "Is that a Texas twang I hear in your voice, son?"

"It is," Jefferson told Colbert with a proud smile.

"By way of El Paso if I don't miss my guess," the former detective said.

Jefferson didn't attempt to hide the fact that he was impressed. "Very good."

"Marty spends a lot of time here, talking to the police officers, police detectives and various people in between. He likes to pick everyone's brain, don't you, Marty?" Cheyenne asked. She thought that what he did, developing an ear for different dialects, was all to his credit.

"Hey, it's what makes life interesting," Marty freely admitted, then turned toward Jefferson and asked the man, "Am I right?"

"Absolutely," Jefferson agreed.

Marty smiled as he looked at Cheyenne. "I think I'm going to like this guy, Detective," he told her. "What are you drinking, son?" he asked the newcomer.

"Water," Jefferson replied in all innocence.

Marty frowned a little. "It's got to be something stronger than that," the man told Jefferson. "The first one's on the house and water doesn't count."

Jefferson paused, then gave Marty the name of a popular light beer.

Marty still looked somewhat disappointed. "Nothing stronger than that, son?"

Jefferson's eyes met the older man's. "No, sir. The light beer will be fine."

Marty raised and lowered his wide shoulders. "Have it your way," he said, resigned, then poured Jefferson a tall mug of light ale. Setting it on the counter in front of the new man, Marty said "Enjoy." And then he looked at Cheyenne. "And what can I get for you, Detective?"

"Nothing, Marty. I'm working tonight after I leave here," Cheyenne told the bartender she had known ever since she had graduated from the police academy and come to work in the Aurora Police Department.

But it was her new partner who was surprised by her statement. "You're working? I thought you were going to go home once you leave here."

She turned toward Jefferson. "I am."

He shook his head. "I don't understand," Jefferson admitted, confused.

"It's called taking your work home with you, Detective," Cheyenne told him. "I've got a couple of files I need to review. Don't bother yourself about that." She knew what he had to be thinking about the matter and she intended to work alone for now. "I brought you here to meet people and to get acclimated. Trust me, there's plenty of time for you to be studying the other side of the coin, McDougall." She turned toward the man behind the counter. "Do me a favor, Marty. Have one of your guys watch over his drink. I want to take him over to meet a couple of the guys," she told the bartender.

"Hey, I can carry my beer, walk and talk all at the same time," Jefferson protested.

"Looks like you've got yourself a regular functioning Ken doll, Cavanaugh," the bartender told her with a dry, amused laugh.

"What's my name, Marty?" she asked the bartender suspiciously, then turned toward her partner to explain why she had asked. "You see, there's a whole bunch of us crowded under the Cavanaugh banner, so if Marty here says 'Cavanaugh,' chances are that he's got a pretty good chance of being right."

Marty regarded the new man. "You'll find that your partner here is pretty damn suspicious about a lot of things most of the time. I don't envy you, boy. Where I come from, this whole ordeal would be known as trial by fire."

"Where do you come from?" Jefferson asked, curious. He wanted to learn as much as he could about the people he was interacting with, and that included the bartender. He prided himself on getting to know people within a short amount of time.

Cheyenne gave the bartender a look, then told her partner, "He's from East LA. Marty here figures that if he puts it that way, he makes it sound more mysterious than it really is."

The expression on Marty's face said that she had just made his point for him.

"I wish I could say you lucked out with this one, son. Tell you what, McDougall, your next drink will be on the house, too. If you ask me, you're going to need that second drink as well," Marty said, then chuckled at what he felt was his own display of wit.

"I think it's time for you to show me how well you can walk and talk and hold a drink at the same time," she told her partner, urging him to move to the rear side of the bar room.

"And the demands will only get more intense from here on in," Marty predicted, shouting after Jefferson's departing back.

"Ignore him," Cheyenne advised her partner.

"Ignore who?" Jefferson asked her innocently.

Cheyenne grinned, tickled. She had been right. She was going to get along just fine with the former Marine and Texas transplant.

Chapter 5

Cheyenne was intent on remaining at the bar for only a little while, then she wanted to go to her home to go over the files she had brought with her. However, she felt obligated to take her new partner around the familiar gathering place and introduce him to people who Jefferson hadn't met earlier in the day. Those were the people who weren't part of the Cold Case Department, but who did contribute to other departments within the precinct. People who were, in her opinion, important for him to know.

She had secretly hoped that she might cross paths with her cousin Valri so that she could introduce the computer wizard to her partner—everyone who worked at the precinct needed the woman's input every now and then for a number of reasons. But she was nowhere to be seen within the establishment.

Cheyenne was aware that the computer wizard kept really long hours at the precinct and then went straight home, but these days there was a reason for that. Being seven months pregnant had a way of taking it out of the poor woman, Cheyenne thought, hoping that one day, she would be able to find out firsthand what that was like.

You won't if you never find anyone, she reminded herself. And seeing as how she kept long hours working in the Cold Case Department, finding someone didn't look like very likely to her at the moment, Cheyenne thought.

Introducing her partner to a couple of old-time detectives, Cheyenne was just about to take her leave when she glanced toward the door. She saw Finley and Brodie, two of her brothers, walking into the establishment. Well, that put her leave-taking on hold, she thought. Cheyenne was well aware that she couldn't leave the place until she properly introduced her brothers to her new partner. It would be an oversight on her part and she knew that they would not allow her to live it down.

All of her siblings were like that, and she had eight of them. If they decided to gang up on her for some reason, she would be done for, Cheyenne thought, even though she could always hold her own. Everything would just grind to a halt.

"Well, I was about to leave you on your own here,

McDougall," she told her partner, turning toward the door, "but those two guys who just walked in happen to be two of my brothers and if I leave before introducing you to them and them to you, I will *never* hear the end of it."

Jefferson appeared surprised by her statement. "I wouldn't say anything about it," her partner assured her.

Cheyenne had her doubts about that. She felt that at bottom the man might just feel slighted by the omission. But it wasn't actually McDougall she was thinking of in this case.

"You might not, but I assure you that my brothers wouldn't let me ever forget it," she told him. Her mouth curved ever so slightly. "They act as if they've taken up permanent residence in my brain. And I have to admit that at times, it actually feels that way."

She beckoned for Jefferson to follow her over to the two men who had just entered the bar. When she made her way over to them, they didn't look surprised to see her. Burrowing between them, she reached up and placed a hand on each of their shoulders.

"Hi, guys, I'm assuming you're here to check out my new partner."

"We just wanted to meet the guy before he becomes history or takes to the hills," Finley told her. Putting his hand out to the new man, he said, "Hi, I'm Finley, one of Chey's older brothers."

"And I'm Brodie, one of her handsomer brothers,"

Brodie said, introducing himself and taking Jefferson's hand once Finley had released it.

Jefferson took each of their hands in turn, giving the brothers warm handshakes and an even warmer smile. "How many brothers do you have?" he asked his partner, curious.

He might have asked Cheyenne for the number, but it was her older brother who answered his question. "This lucky little lady has six brothers," Finley volunteered.

"And there are three sisters in the family," Brodie told him, rounding out the picture.

Finley smiled. "We outnumber our sisters six to three," he informed the new man.

"I take it that your family has some sort of a competition going among you?" Jefferson asked, attempting to gather as much information as possible about the dynamics of his partner's family.

"More or less," Brodie answered. He looked around the bar. "So where are you sitting?" he asked.

Jefferson indicated a table that had been pointed out by Marty when the bartender had served them.

"He was sitting," Cheyenne told her brothers, nodding at Jefferson. "I was in the process of leaving."

Brodie gave her a skeptical look. "You think that's wise?"

She knew exactly what her brother was saying. "If you wanted to, you two would find a way to poison McDougall's mind while I was standing guard right next to him so there's no point in my hovering around, keeping guard over the man now," she told her brothers.

Brodie and Finley exchanged looks.

"I think our sister's been around us too long. There's just no surprising her anymore," Finley said, pretending to sound disappointed about the situation.

Cheyenne gave her brothers a look. "You could act like decent human beings for a change. That would definitely surprise me."

Brodie shook his head, feigning disappointment. "The woman just has no respect for her elders," he said as an aside to Cheyenne's new partner. "I'd definitely watch my back if I were you, McDougall."

"Your back, your front and all the parts in between," Finley told the new man with emphasis, grinning at the image he had just painted.

"I'm not worried," Jefferson told the two brothers, sparing them a glance, then looking at Cheyenne. "I trust your sister."

"This is an even worse situation than I thought," Brodie said to his brother.

Cheyenne frowned dismissively at her brothers. "Very funny, guys."

"And very lucky for you," Finley told his sister, then looked over toward her new partner. "I wish you luck, McDougall. I really do."

"Yeah, me, too," Brodie said, adding his voice to that of his brother's. "You're going to need it. If you find that you need any help or advice," he began to tell her new partner,

"—Just call us, night or day, twenty-four hours a day."

"You two make me sound like some sort of a five-alarm fire that needs to be put out," Cheyenne complained.

"Oh, but you are, Cheyenne, you are," Brodie told his sister with a wide grin, then glanced at her new partner and further emphasized the point. "Trust me, she really is," he told Jefferson with a wide wink.

Cheyenne's partner appeared unconvinced. "If you don't mind, I'd like to judge that for myself," he told the two brothers in a friendly voice.

Brodie and Finley exchanged looks. Brodie laughed, amused by Cheyenne's partner's response.

"Looks like you've got yourself a live one, little sister," Finley said.

"And on that note," Cheyenne announced, looking around at the three men, "I will bid all of you a semi-fond adieu. See you tomorrow. Just make sure you don't damage him, boys. I need to put him to work first thing tomorrow morning."

"You know that you are a tough customer," Finley told his younger sister with a disparaging shake of his head.

"When you're one of nine, you pretty much have to be. It's called self-defense," Cheyenne concluded.

Her brothers regarded her partner with nothing short of heartfelt sympathy. "You know, McDougall, it's really not too early for you to put in a request to be switched to another department," Brodie told his sister's new partner.

Cheyenne shook her head. She knew them too well to take offense. "I'll see you guys around. Give your wives my love—and my complete sympathy."

And with that, Cheyenne made her way to the bar's front door.

She knew that what her brothers were saying was just their way of teasing her and of hazing the new man. She really hoped that they didn't wind up overwhelming McDougall. Piecing together the various clues she had gathered right now on the serial killer or killers was going to be hard enough on him.

When she made her way outside the bar, it was already growing dark. Cheyenne was really happy that her vehicle was not parked down the street or otherwise farther away than it was.

She hadn't realized how tired she was until just this moment. The walk to the car if it were down the block or farther would have taken a great deal out of her.

Great. She was tired and she still had all those files to review and organize. She didn't have all that much to go on. This was all one big hunch on her part.

But something in her gut told her that the three murders she was reviewing were somehow connected, although as of yet, she couldn't quite put her finger on exactly how.

Maybe some alone time in her house would help her sort things out and see her way clear to the answer, Cheyenne thought. Some alone time without a wall of noise throbbing around her. The Cold Case Department was not exactly the quietest place in the precinct. It certainly wasn't designed to foster any deep thoughts about related killings or killers.

Reaching her vehicle, Cheyenne unlocked the driver's-side door. After opening the door, she slid in behind the wheel, then closed and locked the door again. Aurora had a reputation for being an extremely safe city, one of the country's safest for its size for the last twenty years.

Cheyenne liked to think that her law enforcement family had something to do with that.

But despite its reputation, she wasn't one who believed in taking any needless chances. Things had a way of happening when a person least expected them no matter what the circumstances. That was why she was looking at files having to do with serial killers in what could be thought of as being an incredibly safe city.

Trusting to that sort of thing, she thought, starting up her car, was what got people to let their guards down—and that, she knew, backing out of her space, could be a fatal mistake.

The house that Cheyenne lived in was located not too far from the bar, which in turn was not too far from the police precinct.

Driving slowly, she was home in under ten minutes.

She parked her vehicle right at the curb rather

than inside her garage. Once out of her car, she hurried toward her quaint, two story house. She nodded at a neighbor who looked vaguely familiar. The man flashed a smile and then went back to his own thoughts. No words were exchanged and she for one was grateful. She didn't really feel up to having any sort of conversation. She had done enough talking at the bar as well as at the precinct today. She felt all talked out, Cheyenne thought, as she put her key into the lock and opened her door.

She had closed and locked her door when she remembered that she had forgotten to get her mail out of the mailbox down the block, but she was really too tired to backtrack.

Cheyenne shrugged dismissively. She wasn't expecting anything of importance anyway. Anything in her mailbox could wait until morning, she told herself.

At this point, she wasn't all that sure she was going to be able to keep her eyes open to review the files she had bought home. Luckily, she thought, she had remembered to bring those inside with her.

Stepping out of her high heels, Cheyenne moved them aside with her foot, then allowed herself to luxuriate for a moment in the feel of the thick carpet that was beneath her feet. A lot of people, including members of her own family, enjoyed walking on a bare floor. The idea of wood, marble or linoleum left her completely and utterly cold. Literally and otherwise.

Once in her bedroom, Cheyenne quickly changed

out of the formal clothes that she wore to work and into a pair of jeans and a pullover sweater.

Moving back into the living room, she eyed her oversize tan sofa longingly for a second.

But before Cheyenne allowed herself to drop down into the super comfortable cushion, she knew that she needed something that would keep her awake for longer than a few minutes.

Coffee, Cheyenne decided. She needed coffee. Coffee would do the trick and maybe, just maybe, keep her from falling asleep.

Black coffee.

Otherwise, she knew she would wind up getting herself comfortable on the sofa and her eyes would be shut in a matter of moments. And that would seriously hamper her ability to work.

She needed to review the files at least once in order to be prepared for tomorrow. She couldn't have her partner thinking she was a loser on the second day they were working together, she told herself as she went to prepare coffee.

Cheyenne just hoped she wouldn't wind up falling asleep standing next to the counter as she waited for the coffee to finish brewing.

It was a very distinct possibility at this point.

And it had happened to her once.

Chapter 6

Cheyenne wasn't sure if she had imagined it, dreamed it, or if she had had a moment of clarity just before she had wound up falling asleep, but a similarity between the three latest victims that had recently been dug up and subsequently made their way into Autopsy suddenly occurred to her.

Morning found her on the sofa, a couple of pages from the files she had been reading through stuck to her cheeks and a half-formed thought floating in her head.

Cheyenne stretched and yawned as she removed the pages from her skin and placed them back into the proper folders. It took her a few minutes to make sure she had the right papers in the right folders. She wasn't looking to accomplish much, just something to start her off and headed in the right direction.

All murders were unsettling, she thought, but there was something even more so about these bodies that had been dug up and were presently lying in the drawers within Autopsy.

Glancing at her watch, Cheyenne realized that she was running behind the schedule that she had set for herself. Breakfast would have to wait until later, she decided as she hurried to get ready for work. Maybe she could grab something from the cafeteria or from one of the vending machines in the building. But right now, what she needed to do was pack up her files and get going, Cheyenne told herself.

Cheyenne chewed on her lower lip, thinking as she got ready. Maybe she had just imagined those similarities between those murders that had been found once the bodies had been dug up.

Closer examination of the bodies needed to be done to unearth the actual similarities, she thought.

"To be continued," she announced to no one in particular as she dashed into the shower. She was out, dried and dressed within fifteen minutes. The desire to linger was put on hold. Maybe on the weekend.

Dashing out the door, she locked up. Being late to the office would not exactly be setting any sort of decent example for the new guy. There would be plenty of time to fall on her face when he got to know her.

Cheyenne told herself not to dwell on the three bodies that had been unearthed. That wouldn't do her any good in helping advance any theories at the moment. Right now, there were no identifying factors and the faces were not recognizable. The women's facial features had been all but methodically erased.

In her opinion, that alone testified to a great deal of rage and hatred on the part of the killer. Someone felt as if they had been greatly wronged by the persons who'd been killed. There could be no other reason why the killer had lashed out so savagely.

The victims' faces had been destroyed beyond recognition and the fingerprints had been completely removed. Somehow, without any clues to go on, her department would have to come up with the dead people's identities, Cheyenne thought, deeply frustrated.

She really needed some sort of a clue to point her in the right direction.

Cheyenne pulled her car up into its usual space in the police precinct's parking lot, turned off the engine and quickly got out. Taking out the files that she had brought home with her and had been studying, Cheyenne quickly locked up her car behind her, then dashed up the concrete stairs to the precinct's back entrance.

As she did so, she hurried past her cousin Shayla. It took a second for the woman's face to even register in her head, which was already racing a hundred miles an hour.

"In a hurry to get to work?" the blonde detective asked as Cheyenne sailed by her.

The latter came to a skidding halt. "Something like

that," Cheyenne answered, clutching her files against her chest as she flashed a quick smile at her cousin.

"Well, good luck!" Shayla called after her cousin's retreating back.

"Thanks," Cheyenne tossed over her shoulder, resuming her quick pace as she hurried toward the rear precinct door.

Making her way into the building, she decided not to take the elevator but to make her way up the stairwell. In reality, it would be faster.

Cheyenne moved quickly as she made it up to the Cold Case Division. When she reached it, she leaned against the door and paused to let out a rather deep sigh. Cheyenne took in a deep breath, then quickly entered the office.

She could feel her stomach hurting and twisting as it pulled into itself.

Breathing normally now, Cheyenne entered the Cold Case Department. She noted that most of the people who worked there, included Lieutenant Holloway, hadn't gotten in yet.

Releasing a sigh of relief that she had gotten here before her new partner—which was all she actually cared about—Cheyenne got to her desk and all but collapsed into her chair.

The next second, she heard someone entering the office almost right behind her. Cheyenne turned toward the sound. She was surprised to see that her new partner was walking in. The man was carrying two paper bags with him, one in each hand.

Was he that hungry that he was opting for two breakfasts, or was McDougall bringing a friend to the office with him? Thinking it might be the latter, Cheyenne scanned the immediate area, searching for someone she didn't recognize. But there wasn't anyone.

And her new partner was headed in her direction. "So, you came back," she concluded with a smile. "I see that my brothers didn't manage to scare you off," Cheyenne marveled.

"Hey, I always like to see how things wind up turning out," Jefferson told her. He placed one of the bags he had brought in with him on her desk in front of her.

Cheyenne regraded the bag with suspicion. She hadn't asked him to bring in anything in this morning.

"Hey, what's this?" she asked, nodding at the bag. For now, she left it unopened.

"Your brothers mentioned that you like your coffee inky black and that you like to have a toasted bagel for breakfast along with it," he told her.

She stared at Jefferson, attempting to absorb what he was telling her. This was highly unusual in her opinion. "You brought me coffee and a bagel?" she asked him incredulously.

He picked up on her tone and put his own interpretation to her words. "It's not a bribe. I just thought you might want to eat something for some extra energy," he told Cheyenne. "If I got it wrong, it's because I misunderstood what your brothers were telling me. There was a lot to take in and remember yesterday. If I did get it wrong, I can go down to the cafeteria and buy something else or make a quick stop to the local fast-food place and pick up something from there."

She put her hands on the bag to keep the man from taking it away. "No, no, this is fine. As a matter of fact, it's perfect," she amended. She looked at the bag again and said, "This was very thoughtful of you," then added, "I'm very grateful to you for going through all this trouble."

Jefferson shrugged and waved away her words of gratitude. "It's no big deal."

"Oh, but it is," Cheyenne said, contradicting him. "A good working relationship is always a big deal. And feeding me because you figured that I was going to be hungry and punchy at this hour of the morning is really very nice of you." Cheyenne took out her wallet that looked as if it had seen better days. "What do I owe you for this?"

Jefferson didn't hesitate in answering her. "Forgiveness the first time I mess up."

She had no problem with that. "Well, that goes without saying," she responded. "But I meant what do I owe you monetarily?"

Her partner waved his hand at her question. "Don't worry about it. What I paid for it isn't exactly going to break me." Making himself comfortable, he set down his own bag and sat at the desk that had been assigned to him. "As soon as I make short work of this, what do you say that I start working on whatever it is you're working on?" he suggested, then, pausing, thought to ask her, "Just what is it that you are working on?"

She turned toward him because she wanted to see his reaction. "Well, I think that we might have ourselves a genuine serial killer case."

Jefferson seemed instantly interested. "Oh? What makes you think that it's a serial killer who's making the rounds? Is it similar victims, or is he using the same kind of MO or—?"

Cheyenne spread out the three photographs she had managed to amass, the two bodies from the other day and also the most recent one that she had just discovered before she had fallen asleep last night. She decided this might just be a good way to test the new man.

"Tell you what," she said, indicating the photographs. "Why don't you tell me?"

Her partner had finished eating, except for the container of coffee, which he made certain had its lid securely put in place. He carefully studied the photographs that Cheyenne had spread out in front of him.

The women's facial features had all but been erased in the same brutal manner. He couldn't guess at what had been used in order to eradicate the women's features. A hammer? Brass knuckles? He didn't know. In addition, he couldn't even begin to hazard a guess as to what had been used to tie the victims down in each case.

"Well," he began thoughtfully, his face growing slightly pale, "it looks as if all three had been beaten without so much as even a trace of remorse evident. Their faces were heartlessly disfigured, almost erased, as if the killer enjoyed what he was doing. I don't know if whoever did this didn't want his victims recognized, or if he was really angry at his victims and was taking that anger out on them by disfiguring them."

She nodded. "That would have been my guess." And then she hit him with a question he wasn't prepared for. "What makes you think the killer is a male?"

At first her partner was surprised by the question. And then after he gave it some thought, Jeff answered, "I guess I'm guilty of typecasting," and then he picked up the photograph closest to him. "And looking at the photographs again, I don't think the average woman could beat her victim this way without a wave of fury urging her on." He studied the photograph, shaking his head. "You can see by the amount of damage done that the killer appears to be really unhinged."

Cheyenne nodded, glad that her partner saw things the way that she did. "I don't think anyone could possibly argue that serial killers are rational people capable of walking the straight and narrow. I doubt that they are capable of disguising their intentions from the average person for very long."

She sighed, sitting back. "The first thing we need

to do is see if we can identify these victims," Cheyenne said. "Any ideas?"

Jefferson frowned, studying the photographs. "Their faces were destroyed and all trace of fingerprints erased," he reiterated.

"Yes, we already know that," Cheyenne agreed, waiting for the detective to continue.

"Is there some sort of a database for teeth?" he asked her.

She shook her head. "No, no database."

He thought for a moment. "We can try circulating the X-rays of the teeth locally. We might get lucky," he said, watching her expression for a reaction to his suggestion.

She nodded. "Barring any pet theories that might send us looking in the right direction, that might be something for us to try. Good job," she commended her partner. "Why don't you jot down any ideas that you might have about working this case. Who knows, it might even help send us looking in the right direction."

"At the moment, I'm afraid that my brain feels empty," Jefferson confessed.

"Trust me, everyone faced with trying to make rhyme or reason out of the dealings of a serial killer feels like their brain is running on empty at one point or another," she guaranteed. "Sometimes, a lot more than that."

"You've felt that way?" he asked, unable to get himself to believe that, based on what her brothers had told him about Cheyenne. They all seemed pretty proud of her and her ability to deduce things.

"Of course me," she told him. "How do you think I would know that if I hadn't gone through that myself?"

"Because you're being kind?" he suggested.

She laughed out loud at his response. "Don't let any of my brothers hear you saying something like that," she told him. "They'd think I gave you something spiked to drink—or that you've been working too hard and are just hallucinating."

He wasn't buying that. "I got the distinct feeling that your brothers are all very proud of you. Don't forget, you left me alone with them when you went home. They did a lot of talking."

Her eyes narrowed as she looked at him. "I really doubt that they told you they were proud of me," she told her partner.

Her partner felt he had something to counter that opinion. "I don't know, they seemed pretty up on the fact that you are the youngest law enforcement officer in the family to make detective, and in the shortest amount of time."

Cheyenne blinked, surprised. He did sound pretty sincere. "They actually told you that?"

"Well, yeah," he assured her. "How else would I know a fact like that?"

Cheyenne shrugged. "You might have read about it in one of the precinct's newsletters."

"Before I came here, what reason would I have had to read the precinct's newsletters?" he asked.

She was slightly stymied for a moment, then gave in as she nodded her head. "Good point. I guess maybe my brothers are a tad proud of me—not that they would ever say something like that to my face."

"Brothers never do," Jefferson said knowingly. "Or so I'm told."

The admission surprised her. She remembered that she needed to read up on her partner. She still didn't know very much about him. "No siblings?"

The detective shook his head. "Nope."

"Well, I have more than enough to spare," she told him. "You help me solve this cold case and I'll give you one. Maybe even a couple."

His eyes met hers. "I'll hold you to that," he told her with a warm laugh.

She placed her hand in his and shook it. "Deal."

Jeff's eyes smiled at her as he echoed, "Deal."

Chapter 7

He was getting antsy.

He'd really thought he could keep this overwhelming desire that was eating away at him, bit by bit, under control.

But he'd been wrong. He couldn't.

Instead, he could feel that sensation inside him growing and expanding. It was feeding his hunger, making it become all but uncontrollable.

Making it huge.

As Murphy sat in the tiny cubbyhole of a classroom, its very existence an insult to him, he knew he was going to have to do something about this all-consuming hunger eating away at him.

And soon.

Murphy snapped the pencil he had in his hand without even realizing he had done it.

He was envisioning his next victim's neck.

A satisfied smile came over his lips, curving them.

Cheyenne stared at the notes she was rereading for the third time. Possibly even the fourth. It still wasn't making any real sense to her. How could anyone manage to all but erase a person's face the way that the serial killer obviously had?

And more importantly, *why* would the killer do that? To her it was more in keeping with a horror movie than anything real. In her experience, a lot of serial killers were egomaniacs who, while not wanting to get caught, did want the credit that went with the murders that they wound up pulling off. Part of that credit came with others discovering the identity of the people who had been murdered, and how they had been killed. Perhaps not immediately, but eventually.

The murders she had been studying didn't answer *any* questions—they just asked them. And once asked, those questions just continued to linger.

Was this the serial killer's way of taunting the police department, or was there something else going on behind the killer's actions that wasn't clear to her?

Cheyenne sighed. She really wished she knew and could make some sort of sense out of all this confusion.

The newest Cavanaugh detective frowned. This

was *really* frustrating. She honestly had no answers. For now, all she had were questions.

Lots and lots of overlapping questions.

Jefferson looked up, his attention drawn by the sound of her deep sigh.

"You know," her partner speculated, "if you sigh any harder, you're going to wind up blowing that bookshelf down." He jerked a thumb back toward the bookshelf standing behind her.

Cheyenne made a face. "As long as it winds up solving the mystery, I don't care how noisy it winds up being as it crashes," she told her partner honestly.

The detective wound up laughing to himself as he envisioned the bookshelf's fate. "Remind me never to go on a stakeout with you."

She gave her partner a long, penetrating look. "Consider yourself reminded." And then she drew closer to her desk, staring at the paperwork. "Have you managed to make heads or tails out of the killer's reasoning for killing his victims in this manner?" she asked her partner.

"Maybe he didn't have an actual reason," Jefferson guessed. "Maybe what he has is just this overwhelming hunger to kill."

But she shook her head. "Every serial killer has a reason. Doesn't have to make sense to the rest of us," she told the detective. "Just to him. But he still has to have a reason."

But her partner wasn't entirely sold on her reasoning. He eyed her skeptically. "Are you sure about that?"

"I am very sure," she said. And then she pushed herself back from her desk. "I am also getting pretty damn cross-eyed right about now. Do you want to break for lunch?" Time seemed to have gotten away from her.

He let the file folder he was looking at close. "That depends."

"Depends on what?"

"On what you're planning to get for lunch—and where," he told her simply.

She looked up at the detective in surprise. "Are you a fussy eater, McDougall?" She wouldn't have thought that of him, but she was still in the "getting to know you" stage.

Her partner smiled at her. "Let's just say I'm a discerning eater."

Cheyenne returned his smile for the qualification he had just used. "I've got news for you, McDougall. That's kind of the same thing."

For his part, McDougall seemed totally unfazed and unconvinced by her qualification. "If you say so," he told Cheyenne with a quick shrug.

"Tell you what," Cheyenne said, closing down her computer until they returned from lunch. "Why don't you pick the place? I'm assuming that you are familiar enough with the various fast-food places and eating establishments in the immediate vicinity to pick a place that serves food you find enjoyable." She fixed him with a curious look, "Or am I assuming wrong?"

"Well, I'm not exactly a big foodie," her partner began.

"You don't have to be very big on it, you just have to know what you like or what you find tastes good. Unless, of course, it doesn't matter to you what you like. Do you have any actual choices?" she asked, looking into McDougall's eyes.

He felt like he had been reviewing the three files all morning and part of the afternoon. Right now, he suddenly felt weary beyond words, though the words he had been reading and rereading were all dancing right before his eyes.

"I tell you what. Since you're the senior officer here, why don't you pick where we go?" he suggested. "At this point, I'm so hungry it's interfering with my ability to think," he admitted truthfully.

For the time being, Cheyenne put her folder to the side. She decided to try again. "All right, next question. What kind of food do you like? Plain food, Chinese food, pizza, hamburgers, or—" Her voice trailed off as she looked at her partner, waiting for the man to specify some kind of a choice.

Her partner grinned at the question. "I'm fine with 'or,'" he told her.

Cheyenne looked surprised and then laughed. "Well, I certainly can't say that you're a difficult man to please, McDougall." She glanced at her watch. They needed to get moving if they intended to get lunch before lunch wound up turning into dinner. "We've got a little more than forty-five minutes from right now." Patting her pocket to make sure she had her car keys—she did—she told her partner, "If it's all right with you, I'll drive."

"You're the one who knows where we're going," he pointed out. His tone told her that he was surrendering the idea of driving without bothering to contest it.

She flashed a quick smile at him. "In case you're wondering, we're going to this great Chinese restaurant that's been here for as long as the city has existed—maybe even longer."

He nodded as they went out to the elevator. "Sounds good to me. At this point, I'm hungry enough to probably be able to eat logs."

Her expression didn't change. "There's a forest not too far from the city. I could take you there, but you might have to share lunch with a beaver," she whimsically speculated.

Emulating her, Jefferson kept a straight face. "Chinese food will do fine."

Reaching her vehicle, Cheyenne opened all four of the doors simultaneously, then waited for her partner to get in on the passenger side. "Glad we could come to an agreement," she told Jefferson. In less than a minute, she started up her vehicle.

Like everything else, he had come to learn about the immediate area, the restaurant was located not too far from the precinct.

Because it was not the height of the lunch hour,

only a handful of people were waiting to get into the newly redecorated Chinese restaurant.

They were seated within minutes of arriving.

"It's in the back, by the aquarium," the young server apologized as he brought them to their table.

"I find watching fish soothing," Cheyenne told the server by way of letting him know that she was fine with his choice.

"Yeah, so do I," Jefferson said, although he doubted that the server was looking for his approval in this matter. The young guy seemed totally fixated on his partner, the detective noticed. Not that he could really blame the kid. Cheyenne was damn attractive to his way of thinking, Jefferson noted.

Having seated them at the table, the server handed each of them the menus he had brought with him. "I'll be back in a few minutes to take your orders," the boyish server promised, nodding at Cheyenne before he withdrew.

"I think you have a fan," Jefferson whispered to her with a warm smile as the server departed. "I don't think he even noticed that you were with anyone."

She laughed. "He's young," she told her partner magnanimously. "He's probably still trying to feel his way around."

Jefferson smiled broadly as he shrugged his shoulders. "If you ask me, he's got taste."

She wasn't sure how to take that. They had just begun working together and she wasn't able to read him yet. Was he complimenting her, or was there something more to her partner's words than that?

She decided to ask him outright. "Is that a compliment, McDougall?"

"It's an observation," he told her in an offhanded manner. "No more, no less."

She decided to let the matter drop for now. His intention would come to light soon enough and she could put him in his place if she needed to.

"You better get ready to make your choice quickly," Cheyenne told him. "If I remember correctly, they come back to take your order fast here. They like to stand by their service."

Jefferson opened his menu, glanced at it and then looked at her. "What's good here?" he asked.

She rattled off a number of selections, ending with, "Or you can have my favorite, Lobster Cantonese."

Her partner closed his menu and placed it on the table in front of him. "Sounds good to me."

"So, Lobster Cantonese?" she asked.

He partner nodded and smiled. "Yes."

She waited for a second. When he didn't say anything, she pressed, "And?"

"I need more?" he asked her, slightly confused.

She looked at him for a moment, then made a guess. "You don't eat Chinese food very often, do you?"

"I was born and raised eating Mexican food," her partner confessed. "I wouldn't know—Lobster Cantonese," he said, reading the choice from the menu, "from—Moo Goo Gai Pan," he said, reading another selection. "Whatever that is."

She laughed at him. "Trust me, taste-wise you'll like the first one a lot better." She thought for a moment. "I'll have the server throw in egg rolls, fortune cookies and a couple of other tidbits. We'll have you full in no time. Hopefully, we won't get too sleepy to concentrate on work when we finish eating," she told him.

Jefferson thought for a moment. "Okay," he announced, "I'm ready to order."

Cheyenne looked around for their server. The latter was approximately two tables over, bringing a fresh pot of hot tea to the occupants seated there. She waved toward him.

The server glanced over toward Cheyenne's table, nodded and promised, "I'll be right there."

She acknowledged his promise. "Thank you. We are in a little bit of a hurry," she told the server.

He was there to take their order within less than a minute, smiling broadly at Cheyenne. She barely noticed. Her mind was on Jefferson, thinking that their association looked as if it might turn out to be far more pleasant than she had anticipated,

"May I take you order?" the man asked.

She glanced at her partner, then told the server, "Absolutely."

Chapter 8

"I think I might have eaten too much," Jefferson said, groaning slightly as he debated loosening his belt. He decided to leave it alone, although it wasn't really easy.

Cheyenne's partner frowned. They were back in the office, pondering over the information found within the three folders and searching for some sort of a tangible connection between them. They had been working diligently on this cold case for several days now. Lunch today had been over an hour ago.

Cheyenne raised her eyes, looking at him across their desks. "It didn't look as if you had a lot to eat," she said honestly.

Her partner shrugged off her observation. "I guess I'm just not used to eating a lot." He glanced back at the files. At this point, he knew them all by heart. "It would have been nice if this homicidal monster had left us at least part of the faces to look at."

Cheyenne sighed as she stared at the disfigured face in the photograph she was holding. "Agreed, but we have to focus on working with what we do have, not what we *wished* we had."

"And what is it we have?" McDougall asked her pointedly. The way he looked at it, there really wasn't all that much.

She paused, choosing her words carefully. "Well, given the dead bodies' skeletal structures—predominantly their pelvises—I believe that all three of the disfigured victims were older women. None of them were heavyset and given the spread of their hips, the victims were all past the age of childbearing."

Jefferson seemed rather impressed at what Cheyenne had ascertained. "That's pretty astute," her partner told her.

"Not really," she contradicted. "We have a coroner in the family and I pay attention to the things she says, storing it away for use at some future date." Cheyenne looked through the file that was open on her desk for what had to be the umpteenth time and frowned. "I have to admit that right now, no matter how we slice it, we don't exactly have all that much to go on." Sighing, she closed the folder on her desk. "This is no longer the tiny little town that Aurora once was," she lamented, thinking back to the stories that her grandfather had told her when she was a kid. "Now the trail we might choose to follow can wind up leading us to any one of a number of places." Again, Cheyenne felt extremely frustrated.

Jefferson had a feeling that the cases on their desks were not isolated incidents. And he expected there would be more coming. Hopefully not a great many more.

"All these people couldn't have been living in vacuums all to themselves," her partner argued. "Maybe someone related to these women filed a missing persons report, trying to locate them or find out what happened to them."

Cheyenne's expression changed as she inclined her head. Turning the idea over in her mind, she nodded. "Sounds like that might have real possibilities," she agreed, thinking the matter over. "See if you can get hold of anyone in the Missing Persons Department and see if anyone came in recently to file a report on a missing older woman."

"Who do I ask for?" Jefferson asked. "Do you have a name? I'm assuming that there's someone in your family who works in that department." He looked at her from across his desk. "I always found it helps to have someone's name to start out with."

She nodded. "Good point," Cheyenne agreed, complimenting her partner. She thought for a moment. "You could try talking to Travis."

"Travis?" Jefferson repeated. There were a great many Cavanaughs working at the precinct that he didn't know by name yet.

Cheyenne nodded. "Travis," she repeated. "He's my baby brother." She made a note to herself regarding the file she was reviewing at the moment, not wanting to lose her place even though she had gone over it who knew how many times. And then she smiled at her own comment. "We all thought that the Missing Persons Department would be a good fit for him. Travis always had a penchant for being able to find things no matter how misplaced they might be.

"He might turn out to be a huge help to us in identifying these poor faceless victims," she told her partner.

Rolling the idea over in her head, she nodded to herself, picked up the receiver on the precinct's landline and dialed one of the extensions that she knew by heart.

The phone on the other end rang a number of times with no pickup. She was about to hang up and try again later when she heard the receiver on the other end finally being picked up.

"Missing Persons. This is Cavanaugh," a deep voice told her.

She recognized the speaker immediately. Settling back in her chair, she smiled to herself. "Travis? It's Cheyenne."

She heard her brother sigh. "I'll be there, I'll be there," he told her, anticipating her question.

He had caught her completely off guard and she had no idea what her younger brother was talking about. Did he think she was asking him to come to her office? She had no way of knowing what her brother was referring to. She just knew that it didn't make any sense to her.

"You'll be where?" she asked Travis.

"Aren't you calling to remind me to attend Uncle Andrew's birthday party?" he asked his sister.

She'd been so caught up in the serial killer case, Cheyenne had temporarily forgotten all about her uncle's birthday, she thought, stifling a sigh. "I've been so snowed under with this serial killer case and other details," she said, glancing over toward Jefferson, whom she considered to be one of those details, "I forgot all about the party," she confessed, embarrassed at her oversight.

"Oh." Her brother sounded embarrassed for jumping to his conclusion.

"Actually," Cheyenne continued, "that's the reason I'm calling you, Travis."

It was Travis's turn to be clueless as to what Cheyenne was getting at. "You're going to have to give me more of a hint than that, Cheyenne."

It killed her to admit this, but she was not about to beat around the bush regarding the reason for her call. "I need your help, Travis."

"I still need more words, Cheyenne," Travis told his sister.

"Okay, how are these for words?" she asked, getting down to business. "I have got three bodies in the morgue whose faces have been bashed in beyond recognition so we can't make any sort of identifications that would allow us to find out where these people had been and who might have hurt them in this horrible fashion," she said with emphasis.

"Have you tried tracking down their fingerprints through the various records that are available?" Travis asked.

She felt almost insulted that he would even ask her something like that. "Yes, I tried and I'm not exactly a newbie, Travis. And the dead bodies *have* no fingerprints. All of their fingerprints have been erased.

"All we know for sure is that all three victims were older women and they were found buried in various parks in Aurora. Whether the killer brought his victims there to get rid of them, or there was some sort of a message in burying them there,, I don't know. I admit that I am completely stumped over motive and frankly, I can use all the help I can get with these cases. Meaning you," she told her brother pointedly.

"That new partner you got to replace Wade, he isn't any help to you?" Travis asked his sister with a touch of sympathy. He knew that Cheyenne had been upset about her old partner leaving.

"Well, he wasn't trained in mind reading or séances so, so far, he hasn't been able to offer any real help," she said, lowering her voice so that Jeff couldn't overhear her.

He knew that his sister hadn't called him just to kill time. "What would you like me to do?" Travis asked.

"Well, I'm thinking that these faceless victims who had been discovered might turn out being the missing people who had been reported to your department. For now, just send over the names of the people who had been reported as missing and any useful information you might have come across searching for and researching these people."

"Sure thing," Travis agreed. "I'll email it to you. Who knows," he said with a laugh, "we might wind up solving each other's cases."

"We might be satisfied because we find the answers we're looking for," Cheyenne admitted, "but let's face it, we won't be able to tell the families anything positive or comforting about their missing daughters or wives," she concluded sadly, thinking of the possible consequences of this tradeoff.

It was obvious that Travis didn't share his sister's outlook. "Hey, an answer is an answer and we can move on and build from there," he told Cheyenne. "Me, I'll take whatever I can get."

"Well, it looks as if I will have to do the same. Send me the missing persons' names, any details you might have on them and any photos their family or friends gave to you," she told her brother.

"And Uncle Andrew's birthday party this Saturday?" Travis prodded Cheyenne.

"Goes without saying, I'll be there with bells on," she promised.

She heard her brother chuckle. "Nice working

with you, big sister. This is a first for us, isn't it?" he asked as an afterthought.

"But not the last, I hope," she answered. "See you Saturday," she told him just before she hung up the landline receiver.

A couple minutes later, her computer made a noise, announcing that it had received the photos and information that Cheyenne had requested from her brother.

"Hey, McDougall, want to see who we might be looking for?" she asked, beckoning her partner over to look at the photos that had been sent to her. Travis had sent her photos of five different women who had recently been reported missing by their families or friends.

Jefferson came over to stand behind his partner. He studied the different images. "Did your brother happen to send over the important details, like height, weight and age?"

She nodded in response. "Travis is new to the job, but not to the life." She saw that Jefferson was looking at her curiously. "What I mean by 'the life' is that Travis was practically born knowing the important points that go into conducting proper law enforcement and solving crimes. He doesn't even have to stop to think about it. It's just automatic." She smiled at her partner as she pointed out the details on the screen that her partner had asked about. "Here're the important points."

The five photos that had been included all contained descriptions of age, height and weight. Jefferson frowned as he reviewed each very carefully.

"This one sounds like practically a teenager," he said, pointing to the photograph. "I don't think she's one of our faceless victims."

"I agree, but what makes you think that?" Cheyenne wanted to know just how astute her partner could be.

"Because the coroner made that comment about the victims' hips being wide and them having been through childbirth. That means that our victims have families, or did at one point, depending on whether or not those children lived and if anything happened to them afterward."

Jefferson sighed, thinking over his assessment of the case. "There are a hell of a lot of variables to take into consideration."

She smiled as she nodded. "Welcome to the Cold Case Department, McDougall. There's a reason why they call it 'cold' case," she emphasized.

"And yet you're so chipper and upbeat," he couldn't help noting.

"I have to be," she said to her partner. "It's called being defensive. If I wasn't 'chipper' and 'upbeat,' I'd be sitting somewhere in the corner, curled up in a ball, sucking my thumb and trying desperately to find something to help cheer me up," Cheyenne told him.

Jefferson nodded and grinned. "I guess that this is the better alternative."

She looked at him for a moment, trying to make up

her mind, then made a decision. "By the way, are you busy this coming Saturday afternoon and evening?"

"Why? Are you asking me out on a date?" he asked with a grin as he returned to his seat.

"We're not dating, McDougall," she informed him firmly. "We're partners."

"I know that," he answered her dismissively. But then he couldn't make heads or tails out of the question she had just asked about Saturday. "But then why—?"

She came close to dropping the subject, but she knew that her uncle Andrew and her father, both of whom were going to be at the party, would be curious to meet her new partner. Everyone had known and liked her last one. Bringing him to Uncle Andrew's party would go a long way toward answering a lot of questions—and silencing other ones.

"Saturday is my uncle Andrew's birthday. He used to be the chief of police here. Moreover, he throws these incredible parties at the drop of a hat. This one is being thrown *for* him because it's his birthday and I know that my aunt Rose is going to be throwing him one. Would you like to come as my guest? You'll get to meet the rest of my family," she told him as if that would entice him to attend.

"Well, sure," Jefferson said agreeably, "but he doesn't know me."

"This way he will get to know you. And so will everyone else. You'll be more than welcome," she told her new partner.

He smiled broadly. "Then I will definitely come."

She nodded, pleased. "I'll give you the address. Or I can pick you up and take you there since you're new in the area."

"I'd actually appreciate that," he acknowledged. "What can I bring?"

"Just your sunny personality—and a birthday card if you see something that strikes your fancy," she told him.

"I can't go empty-handed," Jefferson protested. "What does your uncle like?"

"That's easy. A united front," she told him. "Okay," Cheyenne declared, picking up one of the folders on her desk. "Back to trying to solve this jigsaw puzzle."

Jefferson said nothing in response. He merely nodded, sighed deeply, then went back to doing as she had suggested.

Chapter 9

Cheyenne felt like she had been going over and over the files, looking for some sort of a hint, some sort of a clue to point her and her partner in the right direction for forever now.

These murders had to have a connection, something in common. Didn't they?

Coming up empty, she sighed for what was probably the dozenth time or so as she reviewed the files that were spread out before her on her desk.

She couldn't get away from the feeling that she was going around in circles and at this point, she almost felt as if she was getting dizzy.

She was missing something.

But what?

Jefferson looked up from the file he was reviewing. All three files had been duplicated so that he and Cheyenne were looking at the same documents, hoping something would strike them.

"You know, you sigh any louder," her partner commented, sparing her a look, "and you're liable to blow me away."

"I didn't know that you were prone to exaggerating," Cheyenne told the man.

Jeff paused to bend over and pick up a few pages that had managed to land on the floor. "I'm not," he said pointedly, taking the pages with him and placing them on her desk, then taking his seat again.

Cheyenne shrugged. Jeff was right. She was overreacting.

"It's just that I feel so frustrated," she complained. "Heaven knows I didn't expect the solution to be a simple one, but I didn't expect it to induce a really throbbing headache, either."

Her partner laughed shortly under his breath. "Tell me about it," he said. About to say something further, the transplanted Texan happened to look up toward the doorway. His attention was drawn to the police officer who was escorting a rather distraught-looking young woman into their office. "Don't look now, Cavanaugh," he said, lowering his voice, "but I think we've got company."

Cheyenne looked toward the doorway. "She might not be headed for us," she commented. "After all, there are other people working in this office."

"You really think that she's not being escorted in

our direction?" Jeff asked, his expression appearing rather skeptical.

"No. She's got that really distraught look on her face," Cheyenne pointed out, studying the woman.

The police officer, Joel Adams, brought the young woman over to Cheyenne's desk. "Detective Cavanaugh, this is Ms. Eve Richardson. I'll let her take it from here," the officer said. And with that, he politely withdrew.

The young woman appeared somewhat embarrassed as well as flustered and at a loss for words. "I'm not really sure if I should even be here," she apologized, looking from one detective to the other. She looked to be in her midthirties and more suited to be relaxing on a cruise ship than filing a report in a police station. The fair-haired woman shifted uncomfortably from side to side.

"Why don't you let us be the judge of that?" Jeff proposed, attempting to do what he could to put the woman who had just walked into their office at her ease. He gestured toward the chair that had been placed next to his partner's desk. "Please, have a seat and tell us exactly what brought you here to us."

Cheyenne was already on her feet, extending her hand to the woman. "Hello, Ms. Richardson. I'm Detective Cheyenne Cavanaugh and this is Detective Jefferson McDougall." She smiled as she said her partner's name. "And if you're wondering about his twang, it's because he's recently moved here from El Paso, Texas. But don't let the accent fool you. There's nothing laidback about him. Detective McDougall is as sharp as they come. Now," Cheyenne said, sitting back down in her chair, "how can we help you, Ms. Richardson?"

Nervous and uncomfortable, the woman was twisting the handkerchief she was holding in her hands, almost making it into a knot. She looked far from at ease with what she was about to say to the two detectives. In fact, she appeared to be at her wit's end.

"You'll probably think that I'm overreacting," the woman told the detectives, looking embarrassed.

"Why don't you tell us what has you so upset?" Cheyenne encouraged. "Then we can tell you if you're overreacting."

The woman took a deep breath, then dived right into the heart of her concern. "I don't know where my mother is."

"Is this something usual for her?" Cheyenne asked. "I mean, do you call each other regularly, or do days, or—"

"Or do weeks go by without any contact between the two of you?" Jeff interjected, doing what he could to attempt to nail the situation down.

The woman blew out a shaky breath. "It all depends. My mother and I—and my older sister—are kind of independent. Liz and I try not to make our mother feel as if we're hounding her every move. To be honest, we gave her a lot of grief about our own independence when we were growing up and in our teens and early twenties. Mom, to her credit, tried to do everything for us. She was like that with us, with our dad until he decided to take off and start a new life somewhere else. And she was definitely like that when it came to our grandmother until Grandma passed away. Mom was all things to all people," the woman told them, doing her best to draw as complete a picture of her mother as she could.

"Initially, after Dad took off, I thought that maybe Mom could use some alone time to just pull herself together. You know, catch up on her life," she said to the detectives, looking from one to the other. The woman smiled sadly. "Mom used the time to go back to school. She threw herself into that, working to support us and herself, until she got her high school diploma. With that under her belt, Mom decided to get her college degree as well."

"Where?" Jeff asked. He was taking notes to draw a fuller picture of the missing woman.

"Locally," she answered automatically.

"How local?" Cheyenne asked pointedly.

"Right here in Aurora College," the young woman was quick to reply. "To be very honest, I was rather pleased at how well things were working out for her and for me. With my mother busy with her job and getting her degree, I realized that I was long overdue for a vacation. So I decided to take one."

"Where did you go?" Cheyenne asked her.

For a moment, the woman's face softened as she thought about the vacation she had spent. "I spent two glorious weeks on a cruise ship. I sent my mother a couple of postcards, asking her how things were going back home, you know, things like that."

"And did she answer you, or acknowledge the postcards?" Jeff asked, trying to get a handle on when communication broke down.

"She didn't say anything specific, but yes, she did say she got the postcards—and that she was happy I was able to get some time away," Eve Richardson said.

Cheyenne studied her expression. "You don't sound entirely sure," the detective commented.

The woman looked disturbed. "Right now, I'm not sure of anything." There were furrows on her forehead. "And there's been all this talk about a serial killer…" Her voice trailed off as she looked at the two detectives for some sort of comfort and reassurance.

"There's no need to let your imagination run away with you," Jefferson said. "Most likely, your mother's just having a good time, or remembering what it was like to be young and carefree, without responsibilities."

"I don't think she was ever young and carefree," the young woman commented. "And definitely not without responsibilities."

Cheyenne felt sorry for the woman. "Parents have a way of surprising us," she told her. "Why don't you give us all the information about your mother that you can—where she worked, what she did, the classes she took at Aurora Valley, things like that. Plus any pictures of your mother you can spare. The more of a complete picture we can put together of your mother, the more of a chance we have of being able to track her down and find her."

Eve Richardson began to look hopeful for the first time since she had walked into the office. "Do you really think that we can?" she asked.

"Thinking negatively won't help," Jefferson told the woman.

"I know," the distraught young woman answered. "It's just that I feel so terribly guilty that I let so much time pass without going to the police about this," Eve Richardson told the detectives.

"Why—specifically?" Cheyenne asked. "You have to have a reason why you feel so guilty about all this," she insisted. Was there something the woman wasn't telling them, or was this just a general wave of guilt she was experiencing?

The woman blew out a shaky breath. "I couldn't wait to go on vacation," she explained.

"There's nothing wrong with that," Cheyenne insisted, waiting to hear the actual reason the woman was so upset.

"And when I came back, I got so busy at work that I didn't touch base with my mother for several weeks. When I finally did," the young woman said. "Mom just wasn't there."

"By 'wasn't there,'" Jeff prompted, "do you mean that she was missing or just going out late at night, or…?" His voice trailed off as he looked at her, waiting for the woman to fill them in on the missing details.

Eve Richardson stared down at her nails, tears forming in her eyes and threatening to fall. "I'm really embarrassed that I can't be more specific than that. I was trying to give my mother her space because I felt that she sacrificed so much for Liz and for me that the best thing I could do was not haunt her every waking moment." The tears that had gathered in her eyes were beginning to fall.

Seeing them, Cheyenne pulled a tissue out of a box on her desk and offered it to the woman.

The distraught woman took it and used the tissue to wipe her eyes. Stifling a sob, she said, "At least, that's what I told myself."

Cheyenne offered her a sympathetic look. "And how's that going for you?" she asked, curious.

Eve Richardson shook her head as she pressed her lips together. "Not well," the woman admitted. There was a hitch in her voice. "Not well at all."

"Well, don't give up yet," Cheyenne encouraged the woman. "Sometimes things have a way of working out when you least expect them to. Trust me, I know."

"I really hope so," Eve Richardson sniffled. She was sounding more and more despondent.

"Okay, let's get practical," Cheyenne told her. "We need the name of the place where your mother worked. Was it a full-time job, or part-time?"

"Part-time ever since she began going back to school. Mom was really intent on getting her degree. She decided that it was high time that she became something," the woman told them. Eve's mouth curved. "Like she needed a degree for that." Amid the hopelessness was a touch of pride as well.

Cheyenne turned a pad over to the woman. "Write down everything you can think of," she urged Eve. "No matter how minor it might seem. Sometimes the smallest detail might wind up being the thing that could very well break the case."

For the first time, she saw real hope entering the woman's eyes.

"Really?" Eve asked the detectives.

"Really," Jeff assured the woman. He took out a card and handed it to the missing woman's daughter. "If you think of anything at all—*anything*," Cheyenne's partner underscored with feeling, "don't hesitate to give me a call. Day or night."

For her part, Cheyenne took out a business card of her own and pressed it into the woman's hand. "The same goes for me," she told Lauren Dixon's distraught daughter.

"And you'll call me? Day or night, you'll call me?" the young woman pressed. "No matter what?"

"No matter what," the detectives said, their voices blending almost in unison.

Finished for the time being with their interview, the two detectives walked the woman back to the officer who had escorted her into the office. He in turn brought her back to the elevator and then downstairs.

With that done, Jefferson went back with Cheyenne to their office. Once there, Cheyenne looked at her partner. They both knew what their next step was going to be—interviewing the people that the missing woman worked with and went to school with.

"Okay," she said, glancing at the list of names that the woman's daughter had handed them, "let's get to this."

"You took the words right out of my mouth," Jefferson told his partner as they got their things and walked into the hallway to the elevator.

Chapter 10

"So do you want to ask the questions or do you want me to?" Jefferson asked his partner.

Cheyenne was surprised by her partner's question. "Why don't we take turns as the questions occur to us?" she suggested after a beat. That seemed to be the better way to go in her opinion.

They had left the precinct and Cheyenne was now driving them to the missing woman's place of work that her daughter had told them about. A Taste of Heaven was a catering restaurant where Lauren Dixon had been working part-time to help her pay for her college education ever since she had gotten her high school degree. According to her daughter, the woman had worked there until she had inexplicably disappeared.

Jefferson nodded. "That sounds good to me," he told Cheyenne. Wanting to make sure that they were on the same page, Jeff asked his partner, "Exactly what information are we going to go with on this missing woman?"

Cheyenne thought for a moment, reviewing what had been said. She didn't want them to get ahead of themselves or say too much to begin with. "Well, according to her daughter, Lauren Dixon is almost sixty-one years young and she's eager to start, as Eve Richardson put it, the second half of her life." She found that a very admirable sentiment.

"The second half of her life," McDougall repeated, amused. "Does that mean that the woman is planning on living until she's one hundred and twenty-eight years old?"

Cheyenne shrugged. All things considered in this day and age, that was not a total impossibility.

"Who knows? Science and medicine are making tremendous strides these days. Anything could be possible." She could almost feel the detective staring at her profile. She spared him a quick glance. "What?"

Jefferson laughed. "You really are an optimist, aren't you?"

She was obviously amusing him, Cheyenne thought. But that wasn't exactly her goal.

"I don't see a point in wallowing in dark thoughts," she told him. "Dark thoughts will find you soon enough if that's the intention."

Cheyenne's new partner nodded. "Can't argue with that, I guess."

Sure he could, she thought. Out loud she declared, "Good," tossing the comment in her partner's general direction.

A Taste of Heaven was located in a small, neat-looking little shopping center that was located in the southern section of Aurora. Since it was a weekday, there was plenty of available parking at this time of day.

Pulling up into the first available space she found, Cheyenne set the hand brake and turned off the engine, then got out of her vehicle.

Jefferson was right there next to her.

"Looks like a nice place to work," he commented, looking up at the freshly painted single-story restaurant.

"Looks can be deceiving," she told him. "But offhand, I'd have to agree that you're right."

Cheyenne led the way into the restaurant. As she pushed open the door, an old-fashioned bell hanging overhead made a tinkling sound, announcing their entrance. She caught herself thinking that it really did seem like a rather charming place.

"I'll be right with you," a heavyset woman called out, writing something down on an electronic pad she was holding.

Jefferson looked around the restaurant, trying to visualize it through the missing woman's eyes. "It really does look like a nice place to work," he reiterated to Cheyenne.

She really wasn't all that willing to agree with him yet. She had a very healthy sense of skepticism. "That all depends on the pace they expect you to keep up," she told her partner. "Some places appear welcoming on the outside but are conducted like sweatshops from within."

The other detective shrugged, thinking the judgment to be a bit harsh. "I'll take your word for it."

At that point, the woman with the electronic pad approached them. There was a broad pasted-on smile on her lips. "Now then, what can I get for you folks?" she wanted to know, her sweeping glance taking them both in.

"We're here to ask you a few questions about one of the people who works at your restaurant," Cheyenne told the woman as she flashed her police credentials. Jefferson had taken out his silently. "A Lauren Dixon."

The woman's smile faded and she shook her head. "I'm afraid Lauren doesn't work here anymore. It's a shame," she commented, "because she was a really good worker. She was here full-time for years, then went part-time," the woman, whose name according to the name tag she wore was Cecilia, told them.

"Did you fire her?" Cheyenne asked the woman bluntly. She felt that was the quickest way to get the woman's story out of her.

"In theory I guess you could say that," Cecelia answered.

"Would you care to explain that?" Cheyenne asked.

The other woman just shrugged almost helplessly in response. "She just stopped showing up one day. It was kind of ironic, really," she told the two detectives, "because I was about to give her a raise. But like I said, Lauren just stopped showing up. One of the other women who work here speculated that she probably got caught up in going for her college degree. Undoubtedly she had bigger things in mind than just working in a restaurant." The woman, who Cheyenne assumed was the manager, frowned. "I have to admit that I'm ticked off with her for just walking away like that without giving me any notice, but ultimately I do wish her luck."

"Even though she just walked out on you like that?" Jefferson asked, trying to reconcile the two stories.

"What can I tell you? From the very first day she started working here, Lauren always inspired nothing but feelings of goodwill and loyalty. Until she inexplicably decided to play hooky, she was always the most dependable, the most loyal person I ever encountered." Cecilia sighed. "I just know that I'm never going to find anyone else like her," the manager lamented.

"Do you have any idea why she would just take off the way she did? Maybe she had an argument with one of the people she worked with or...?" Cheyenne's voice trailed off, leaving a space for the manager to fill in a reason if she was able to do that.

The restaurant manager shook her head, appearing at a total loss.

"Believe me, I did ask around. If there was some sort of an argument that caused Lauren to just walk out, no one here knows anything about it, or at least they aren't admitting to it. Besides, in my opinion, that sort of thing just wasn't her style. I think I knew her well enough to say that if there was a problem, she would have dealt with it, not just walked out without so much as a backward glance." The restaurant manager just sighed. "If you ask me, this is a really big mystery," she admitted.

"Do you think that something could have happened to her?" Cheyenne asked the woman.

"Like what? A car accident?" the manager asked. "I think I would have heard about it," she told them. "Or one of the other girls would have read or heard about it and told me."

"Maybe someone took her prisoner or did something to her," Jefferson quietly suggested, watching the woman's face to see what her reaction to that would be.

It was clear that the very idea horrified the restaurant manager. Her eyes widened. "You don't really think that happened, do you?"

"We're not about to rule anything out for certain until we check out every possibility," Jefferson told the restaurant manager.

"If you hear anything or think of anything," Cheyenne told the woman, taking out her business card and putting it into her hand, "please don't hesitate to call us—day or night," she emphasized.

The woman stared at the card in her hand, as if committing what was written on it to memory. "I will," she whispered, more to herself than to the police detectives standing before her.

Satisfied that the manager was taking the instruction to heart, Cheyenne continued. "If you don't mind, we'd also like to talk to the other people that Lauren knew and worked with."

"Of course, of course," the restaurant manager agreed wholeheartedly, bringing them over to the women who were working the counter and the register. The two women had been covertly watching them since they had begun talking to the manager.

"We'll keep it brief," Jefferson promised, thinking that the mere idea of questioning these women might wind up scaring them off.

An hour and a half later, Cheyenne and her partner were no closer to discovering just what had happened to Lauren Dixon, what had caused her to disappear off the face of the earth, than they had been when they'd first walked in. No one Lauren had worked with had any sort of clue as to what had happened to her.

"You want to go to the junior college and question the people there? Maybe they have an idea about what happened to Lauren Dixon," Jefferson suggested to his partner.

Cheyenne unlocked her car and waited for him to get in on his side. "Well, we do have a few hours of daylight left, we might as well use it," she speculated. Heaven knew that this mystery was not about to solve itself, she thought.

"Do you know what class or classes Lauren was taking at the college?" Jeff asked as he got into Cheyenne's car. "In other words, where do we start?"

"We start at the registrar's office," she told her partner. "With any luck, Lauren Dixon won't have been enrolled in too many classes. That'll keep the number of people we need to talk to and interview hopefully down to a manageable minimum." Cheyenne crossed her fingers for a second, holding her hand up in the air, before starting her vehicle and taking the wheel.

Aurora Valley College was located along Aurora's old main thoroughfare. Initially it had been an incredibly small college. It had grown over the last twenty-five years, almost doubling in size as the years went on.

Fortunately, the registrar's office had remained in the exact same location it'd been since the school was erected.

Cheyenne didn't hesitate when it came to parking her vehicle. She pulled the car up into an area meant just for visitors rather than students or instructors.

Turning off her engine, she told her partner, "We'll

start here. Hopefully, we'll have better luck than we had with Lauren Dixon's place of work."

"You know there is a possibility that Lauren Dixon might have just gotten fed up with her life and decided to take off," Jefferson said.

"From everything her daughter told us, that woman was not the type to just take off on a whim. Lauren sounded extremely dependable. That meant she would have told one of her daughters or one of her friends what she was planning on doing. Given the personality Eve said her mother had, she was not the type to disregard people's feelings and just do whatever she wanted to on a whim."

Jefferson followed his partner as she led the way to the registrar's building. "Do you think Lauren Dixon is one of the women lying in our morgue?"

"I sincerely hope not," Cheyenne answered her partner with feeling. "But right now we honestly have no way of knowing." Pausing, she stopped outside the door and read the words written on it that declared it was the main registrar office. "Looks like this must be the place," she said to her partner just before she opened the door.

A harried-looking woman looked up as Cheyenne and Jefferson walked in. She made no effort to disguise the sigh that escaped her lips.

"May I help you?" the woman asked in voice that indicated she was clearly stressed out.

Cheyenne and Jefferson took out their credentials almost simultaneously and held them up for the woman's viewing.

"Detectives Cavanaugh and McDougall," Cheyenne told the woman. "We're with the Aurora police's Cold Case Department. We would like to speak to someone about one of the students who was enrolled at Aurora Valley College."

"Which student?" the woman asked, addressing her question to Jefferson.

"Her name is Lauren Dixon," Cheyenne said, answering the woman behind the counter, who stopped what she was doing and went to a computer located on the other side of the room.

"What was that name again?" the woman asked.

"Lauren Dixon," Jefferson repeated. "We were told that she was enrolled here this semester."

"We don't have semesters, we have quarters," the woman corrected with a flicker of a smile as she pulled up the current registration lists and looked up the missing student's name. "Lauren Dixon. Is that the traditional spelling?" she asked. This time she addressed her question to both of them. "These days, everything is subject to some fancy change or other," the woman explained.

"Traditional spelling," Cheyenne answered. Then, as she spelled the missing woman's name for the clerk's benefit, she also held up the photograph the woman's daughter had given them so that the clerk had a visual aid. "This is what she looks like, in case she might have had a reason to come in recently."

Cheyenne hoped that the photo might jar the clerk's memory if that were the case.

There was no sign of recognition in the woman's eyes as she looked at the picture. She shook her head.

"Sorry. This office sees a lot of foot traffic during each quarter. When was she supposed to have been registered here?" she asked.

"This quarter," Jefferson said, going by their most recent information, then added, "Last quarter for sure."

The woman smiled at him before going through the listings. "Lauren Dixon, you said?"

"Yes," Jefferson answered the woman, watching her face.

After a few moments, the woman located the name. "She signed up for two classes this quarter, both given in the evening."

"Could you give us the names of the courses and the instructors who are teaching them?" Cheyenne requested. She was still hoping they might be able to jar someone's memory.

"I'll be happy to, but Professor Jon Murphy isn't in today. His class is in the lecture hall. Dr. Joanna Barnes, the other instructor, is in, though. One out of two isn't bad," the woman told Jefferson, flashing a smile at him.

"When is Professor Murphy in?" Cheyenne asked.

"He might be in tomorrow. He'll definitely be in on Monday. But like I said, Dr. Barnes is in tonight. She's teaching," the woman said.

"If you give us her room number, we'll be out of your hair," Jefferson promised.

The woman wrote down the class and room number and then handed the sheet of paper to Jefferson. "You can be in my hair anytime," she told him with a wide, inviting smile.

Avoiding the woman's eyes, Jeff folded the paper and then handed it to Cheyenne. "Thank you," he told the woman, then followed his partner out of the building.

Chapter 11

"I think that woman in the registrar's office would have been more than happy to take you over to the professor's lecture hall," Cheyenne observed.

"Well, to be honest, I got the feeling she was more than happy to be rid of us," Jefferson emphasized, calling an end to the conversation.

Cheyenne had left her vehicle parked right outside the office. He stopped right next to it. "Do you want to drive over there, or should we just walk?"

Glancing at the paper the woman in the registrar's officer had given them, Cheyenne shook her head. "This is close enough for us to walk to. Class starts on the hour. With luck, we can catch Professor Barnes just as she arrives and before she starts to teach her class. That way we'll be able to ask her a few questions about Lauren Dixon."

"You've got this all worked out, don't you?" her partner asked. There was a note of admiration evident in his voice.

"I used to attend this college," she told him, then amended, "at least, Aurora Valley was my starting point."

"Your starting point," he repeated as they continued to walk. "What happened?"

That was easy enough to explain. "The second I got my grades up, I transferred to the University of Aurora." The latter had a lot more to offer. She saw the question in Jefferson's eyes and quickly explained the difference to him. "Aurora Valley is a two-year college. The University of Aurora is a four-year college and rather well regarded."

Her partner nodded. The names of the universities were all new to him. "Consider me educated," he told her. He looked at her profile and asked, "Did you like going to Aurora Valley?"

She shrugged slightly. "It had a nice, homey feel. It was a good place to get your feet wet starting a college education," she told him. "It was definitely not too overwhelming or intimidating a place to start out."

The words *to start out* stuck in his head. "But you didn't stay the full two years."

Cheyenne shrugged again, then grinned. "I suppose that I wasn't overwhelmed or intimidated for very long."

Jefferson nodded. "I wouldn't think that you would be. You don't strike me as the type to be intimidated." He saw his partner stopping before a large round building. This had to be the lecture hall, he thought, but just to be on the safe side, he asked, "Is this where Professor Barnes is teaching?"

Cheyenne smiled at him in response. Some of the landscaping had changed at Aurora Valley, but not this area. "Yes, this is it," she confirmed. "We've got a little less than fifteen minutes before class starts."

He opened the door for her, but before she walked in, he told her, "I think that you should do all the talking."

His statement took her by surprise. "Any particular reason why?"

"Yeah," he confirmed with a smile. "You can talk a lot faster than I can, which means you can get a lot more words out," Jeff told her.

She gazed at him a little uncertainly. "You know, I don't know if I should be flattered or insulted by that comment."

"It's just a given," he told her. "But if you're torn and waffling between leaning in one direction or the other, I'd say you should go with being flattered. I didn't mean it as an insult."

"Flattered it is," Cheyenne told him with an amused, agreeable smile as she walked into the hall ahead of her partner.

The thing that first struck Cheyenne was how dimly lit the lecture hall was. She paused, as did her partner, then took baby steps into the hall, making sure that she didn't trip.

None of the students appeared to be there yet and the lighting took some getting used to. Adjusting to it definitely took at least a couple of minutes.

Cheyenne remained standing at one spot for a couple of seconds before she finally took a tentative step forward. She could feel her partner doing the same thing. He was following her lead. For a moment, she thought he would take her arm to help keep her steady and she had to admit, she rather liked the idea, although she wasn't about to say it out loud.

The dark-haired woman sitting at the desk on the raised platform looked up even though the people who had walked in had made absolutely no noise to alert her.

"Dr. Barnes?" Cheyenne asked, moving forward. Her partner didn't miss a step and was right there behind her.

Curiosity entered the professor's brown eyes as they swept over the strangers who had just walked in. "Yes?"

Cheyenne took out her wallet and flashed her identification for the woman to see. "We're detectives Cavanaugh and McDougall with the Aurora PD," she said, nodding at her partner, "and we're looking into the possible disappearance of one of your students."

The professor rose and came around her desk in order to look at the credentials. Verifying their authenticity, the professor nodded.

"You're talking about Lauren Dixon, aren't you?" she asked. A slight frown graced her lips.

That struck Cheyenne as a really good guess on the professor's part. In a class of this size, the instructor wouldn't have been aware of a missing student unless there was a good reason for it. This Lauren Dixon had to have made an impression on the lecturer and possibly the rest of her class.

"As a matter of fact, we are." The professor tilted her head, looking at the detectives quizzically. "How did you know that?" Cheyenne asked.

"I've had other students drop out or stop showing up to class during the school year, of course, but Lauren always struck me as being very conscientious about attending classes. When she stopped showing up to class, I actually got her home number from the registrar's office and called her to see what had happened and why she'd stopped coming."

"And what did you find out?" Jefferson asked, urging the instructor to get on with her story.

Professor Barnes shook her head. "Nothing. I didn't find out anything. Lauren never answered. I called her a couple of times and then I just gave up. I decided that if taking my class was important enough to her, she would eventually turn up." She looked at the two detectives. "Wouldn't she?" the instructor asked them, clearly wanting the detectives to agree with her.

"If she could," Cheyenne answered the professor guardedly.

The professor's brow furrowed as she looked from one detective to another. "Meaning that she can't?" Barnes questioned, looking somewhat unnerved.

"That's what we're trying to ascertain," Cheyenne told the instructor honestly.

"Did she just take off?" Barnes asked, attempting to get a handle on the situation.

"That would be the simplest explanation," Jefferson said. "If you don't mind, Professor, when your students file in, would you possibly be able to point out the ones who you knew were friendly with Mrs. Dixon? Maybe they can tell us something that might be able to help our search."

The professor nodded. She looked more than willing to help find the missing woman. "When they come in, I can ask the class if any of them were friendly with Ms. Dixon. To be honest, I really don't know who she socialized with and who she didn't, but I can certainly ask. Maybe someone in the class can give us some insight into the situation." The professor was obviously curious and appeared as if she felt she was facing an honest-to-goodness mystery.

"Any help you can provide us with will be more than gratefully appreciated," Jefferson told the professor.

The woman seemed to brighten up right before their very eyes in response to Jefferson's statement. "I am more than happy to do my part in finding Mrs. Dixon. It's really hard to believe that in this day and age someone can just disappear off the face of the earth this way," the professor lamented. "We have to be able to find her."

Just then the instructor was interrupted by the sound of raised voices as students began walking into the lecture hall.

Most of the students looked to be in their early- to midtwenties, Cheyenne judged, watching them filing in. Those students, she thought, would have little to nothing in common with the missing woman. But she noticed a few students, women for the most part, were the missing Lauren Dixon's age, or close to it. With any luck, Lauren had shared confidences with these people. If she and Jefferson talked to the students, they might be able to find out something pertinent that would help them discover what might have happened to Lauren Dixon.

As the ninety-five or so students filed into the auditorium and took seats that could be described as being around the lecturer, many of them threw curious glances in the strangers' direction.

The professor waited for her students to be seated before she addressed them.

"Ladies and gentlemen, you might have noticed that we have visitors in our lecture hall." She looked around the room, making eye contact with a great many of her students. "They are investigating what happened to one of your fellow students. According to her family, Lauren Dixon, the lady who always sat up front and to the left side—" the professor pointed the area out "—has been missing from her home. They are hoping that one of you might be able to provide a clue as to where she might have gone. Do any one of you have any idea as to what might have happened to Lauren Dixon or where she might have gone?"

There was a low murmuring of voices as this was discussed among several of the older students.

"Can any of you provide us with any insight into Ms. Dixon's dealings?" the professor asked.

There were more voices murmuring, but no one seemed as if they had any information to volunteer. Nor did they appear to be holding back a secret.

It was a case of no one knowing anything, Cheyenne thought.

Cheyenne decided to try to appeal to the students' sense of sympathy.

"Professor Barnes has our cards and can get in contact with us, If anyone knows anything at all, no matter how small it might seem, we would really appreciate you letting us know. Put yourselves in the family's position," she said to the students in the lecture hall. "What if this was one of you and your family was going through hell, wondering what had happened to you and why no one had any insight into what might have happened to their loved one? The slightest hint you can provide us with will be greatly appreciated," Cheyenne said, scanning the faces of the students sitting in the lecture hall.

"She kept to herself, but I know she liked the material we were assigned to read," one older student volunteered, speaking up.

Cheyenne did her best not to show her disappointment over this lack of insight. Instead, she nodded and thanked the person who had volunteered this meager piece of information. "Thank you."

"Does anyone have anything else to add?" Jefferson asked. He scanned the faces that appeared to be focused on him and his partner, but no one seemed to have anything more to add.

And then one of the older students raised her hand. When Cheyenne called on her, the woman added, "I know she liked this class more than she liked going to her other class, even though she liked that reading material, too."

"What class was that?" Jefferson asked before his partner had the chance. He wanted to be sure they were on the same page and that the student was talking about the same class.

"Professor Murphy's class," the woman told them, confirming the impression.

"Professor Murphy's class?" Cheyenne asked. She was vaguely familiar with the name, but she didn't really know the instructor. She told herself that she really needed to get her hands on the present class schedule. "Murphy" was a common enough name. Maybe the college had more than one Professor Murphy.

"He lectures on he development of murder mysteries throughout the ages," another one of the students answered, raising her voice. "I take that class, too. Professor Murphy makes it sound so realistic, I have to admit that he gives me the creeps," the woman confided. She shivered to emphasize her point.

"Why is that?" Jefferson asked.

The woman sighed, then said, "He takes such relish in going over all the fine points of murdering a victim," the woman emphasized. "I swear his eyes light up."

Cheyenne exchanged glances with her partner. "We need to talk to the professor as soon as we can. Where can we find him?" she asked Professor Barnes, hoping to get a different answer than the one provided by the woman in the registrar's office.

"He's got a class on Monday," the professor told them, repeating what they're already gleaned from her colleague.

That wasn't good enough, Cheyenne thought. She was experiencing one of those famous Cavanaugh gut feelings several of her uncles and cousins liked to talk about. They needed to pin this man down. "We need to speak to Professor Murphy before Monday. Which means that we're going to have to go back to the registrar's office so we can get the man's home address," she told Professor Barnes as well as her partner. She turned toward Professor Barnes. "Unless, of course, you have it."

But the instructor adamantly shook her head. "Sorry. Professor Murphy and I don't socialize off-campus. We hardly socialize *on* the campus," she emphasized.

"Any particular reason for that?" Cheyenne asked the woman.

The professor turned her back toward her students in order not to be overheard. "Between you and me, the man has a way of looking at you that seems to go straight through you. He makes me shiver," she confided to the two detectives. "I know I'm not being very fair, but very frankly, I am much too busy to care about that. I have too many students to juggle, too many papers to grade."

"We understand," Jefferson told her. "Thank you for your help and for allowing us to invade your lecture hall, Dr. Barnes. But right now, if we want to catch the woman in the registrar's office before she leaves for the night, I'm afraid we really need to get going."

"Of course, of course." The professor walked out with Cheyenne and her partner. "If you think of anything else that you might need, don't hesitate to let me know," she said, and to the professor's credit, she addressed her words to both of the police detectives, not just to Jefferson.

Cheyenne nodded her head. "We'll be sure to do that," she promised the professor, then turned toward her partner. "Okay, McDougall, let's get going," she urged the man.

She noticed that her partner nodded at the instructor as they left. Several of the students noticed as well—and sighed as their thoughts appeared to take off, creating potentially interesting scenarios.

Chapter 12

When they approached the registrar's office, Wanda, the woman who ran it, was just in the process of locking up and going home. Jeff quickened his pace, managing to get in the woman's way before she was able to leave.

"We need a word—Wanda," he called out, belatedly remembering the woman's name.

Startled, the woman turned around. When she saw who was calling to her, she smiled and waited for the detectives to approach her.

"I'm in a hurry. It's my night to make dinner," she explained, appearing to be rather antsy about what she was telling them. Smiling, she told Jefferson, "You're going to have to talk fast."

Jeff grinned. "Fast talking is my partner's specialty," he told the woman as he looked at Cheyenne.

The woman raised one eyebrow as she looked in Cheyenne's direction. "Okay, so talk," she urged.

"We need you to give us Professor Murphy's home address," Cheyenne told the woman.

Looking extremely apologetic, Wanda shook her head. "I'm afraid that the college isn't at liberty to release that kind of information."

"You said that Professor Murphy wouldn't be back at the college until Monday," Cheyenne reminded the woman.

"He won't be—" Wanda began.

"I'm afraid we can't wait until Monday," Cheyenne told the woman. "We need to question Professor Murphy as soon as possible." She paused, then added, "The matter might involve a murder victim—"

Wanda held up her hand to stop the flow of conversation before it could get too far. "The professor isn't home," she told them.

"Why? Where is he?" Jeff asked, putting the question to her.

Wanda shook her head. "All I know is that this is the anniversary of his aunt's death and he said something about planning on visiting her grave."

"Which is where?" Cheyenne prodded. Wherever it was, she and Jeff could stake out the area and wait for the professor to show up. Who knew? It might even wind up providing them with an important clue. At least she could hope.

But Wanda shook her head. "I honestly haven't a clue," the woman confessed. "He never told anyone where it was."

"Who would have that information?" Cheyenne asked the woman.

She shrugged her shoulders, at a loss. "I really don't know. Professor Murphy doesn't talk to anyone that I know of. To be honest, the professor gets here just before his class starts and then he teaches his students." The wind was picking up and Wanda drew her collar up and pulled her coat closer around her to shut out the cold. "Sometimes, if the students have any questions for him, Murphy does stay after hours. But that really doesn't happen all that often.

"Most of the time, from what I hear, the students are in a rush to leave and go home themselves. The professor's class is the last one of the evening. It is pretty late right now. And since there's no class tonight—" the woman gestured around the area "—there isn't anyone around for you to ask."

"And you really don't have his address on file?" Cheyenne pressed.

"We do," Wanda admitted, "but like I said, it is a privacy issue and I am not able to release it. Besides, even if I did, most likely the professor is not going to be there anyway."

Jefferson's eyes met the woman's. "Even so, keeping that in mind, could you give us the address anyway?" he asked.

"I would really like to," Wanda told him in all

sincerity. "But I can't give it to you without risking losing my job," she said honestly.

"We wouldn't tell anyone," Cheyenne promised, although she had a feeling that really wouldn't do the trick and change the woman's mind.

"Well, maybe you wouldn't, but if the professor somehow got wind of his address getting out, like I said, I would lose my job." She lowered her voice as she shared how she felt about the situation. "Professor Murphy is *not* the forgiving type and I really need my job. I am the only source of income for my widowed mother as well as for myself." She attempted to shift the detectives' focus away from the topic. "Professor Murphy said he would be in early on Monday. Well, early for him," she clarified.

"And that would be—?" Cheyenne prodded, wanting the woman to pinpoint a time.

Wanda thought for a moment, wanting to be as accurate as possible. "On Mondays Professor Murphy is in at four," the woman told the two detectives.

Cheyenne exchanged glances with her partner. "I guess we'll be here on Monday right before four o'clock," she told Jefferson.

"I wouldn't suggest getting here too much before four," Wanda cautioned, then said, "I've never known the professor to come in early."

Jefferson laughed drily under his breath. "I think I'm in the wrong line of work."

Cheyenne made no comment until they left the building. "Do you get a sense of satisfaction when you solve a crime?" she asked her partner as they walked out and headed back to her car.

"Well, yeah," her partner said, wondering what she was getting at. "I wouldn't be here if I didn't."

"Then I'd say you're in exactly the right line of work," she told him. "There's no satisfaction in shirking your responsibility—if you did that sort of thing."

Jefferson thought for a moment. "I guess you're right."

She grinned at him. "Thanks. I generally am. Okay," Cheyenne declared. "Let's call it a night. I'll bring you back to your vehicle in the precinct parking lot. Tomorrow we can look into seeing if either of the other two faceless women has an identity we can actually attempt to pin down. Maybe we'll get lucky," she told him. "In any case, we have my uncle's party to go to on the following day."

Jefferson had almost forgotten all about the party she had invited him to. "Oh, about that," her partner began.

Cheyenne glanced in his direction. "No," she told him flatly.

"No?" Jefferson asked.

"No," Cheyenne repeated, then explained, "The time to wiggle out of having to attend my uncle's birthday party has come and gone, Jefferson. My uncle Andrew wants to meet you and this birthday party for him is going to be the easiest way to accomplish that. Actually," she amended, "my whole family is looking forward to meeting you."

"I've already met some of them," Jefferson reminded her. For some people, he thought, that would have been enough.

"You met *a couple* of them," Cheyenne pointed out. "But definitely not anywhere near all of them. You have to remember that the Aurora police force is actually more like the family business than anything else. So no more arguing, McDougall. You're coming, no ifs, ands, or buts," his partner told him forcefully. Her eyes all but pinned him in place. "Have I made myself clear, McDougall?"

He laughed as he absorbed his partner's words. "Crystal," he told her, then asked, "Has anyone ever told you that you're really bossy?"

"You want that answer alphabetically or chronologically?" she asked her partner.

"Then I take it that the answer to that is yes, huh?" he asked her.

"Well, except for a few cousins in that group, the answer is that it's mostly my brothers saying so," Cheyenne answered, lifting her shoulders, then letting them drop in a casual shrug. "Sorry. I'm afraid that you're not being very original."

"I wasn't trying for originality," her partner admitted. "I was just trying to make a point." And they both knew what that was, he thought.

"Consider it made," she answered with a small, soft smile. "Look, for this partnership to work, McDougall, we always have to be honest with one another. No tiptoeing around important points, and just practicing basic honesty," she emphasized. And then she raised her eyebrows. "Have I made myself clear?"

"Well, if you want honesty…" her partner began, doing his best to try to get his point across.

"I do, but we're moving away from that subject now," she told him. "Besides, you wouldn't want to insult the rest of my family. As a rule, they're not a vindictive bunch of people, but they don't take well to having their own insulted and the first thing that would come to mind for them is that you're my partner and you're shining me—and them—on by not attending the birthday party if you choose to skip it."

Jefferson nodded. "Well, I certainly wouldn't want to do that," he assured Cheyenne. And then he smiled at her. Cheyenne caught herself thinking that the man really did have a very nice smile. "To be honest," her partner told her, "I really wouldn't mind meeting your family all at once. I just wanted to see what you'd say if I told you I wasn't going to show up."

They got to her car and got in. "Well, for one thing, I wouldn't recommend you flashing that sense of humor around them. It might not be taken well," she warned him.

"Duly noted," he told her.

It took only a few more minutes for Cheyenne to arrive at the precinct parking lot. Because of the time of day, the lot was for the most part empty.

Entering it via the back way, she was able to pull up next to her partner's car before stopping her vehicle.

"Tomorrow, I'll give you my uncle's home address, but that'll be strictly for your own information. I've decided to pick you up at the apartment you're renting and take you to my uncle's house myself. It'll be easier for you that way."

"You don't have to do that. I can get myself there," Jefferson promised her.

"I know that," she answered. "But this way, you can enjoy a few drinks without worrying about driving with a higher alcohol content than you should have."

"Don't worry, the new guy has no intention of getting drunk," he assured her.

But Cheyenne wanted to cover all the bases, just in case. "Well, this way the 'new guy' won't have to worry if he decides to have one too many—or more."

He didn't want her getting the wrong idea about him. "I appreciate that, but—"

Cheyenne pulled her lips back into a wide smile. "No 'buts,' partner," she told him, then glanced at her watch. "Time for me to get going, but for that to happen, you need to get out of my car." She looked pointedly at the passenger door.

Jefferson nodded. "And that would be my cue," he declared, his hand on the door latch. He pushed it open. "See you tomorrow, partner."

Cheyenne nodded. "Same time, same place," she said, her eyes sparkling.

And with that, Cheyenne took off feeling rather accomplished.

She needed to get her sleep. Tomorrow already looked as if it had all the makings of another very long day. She intended to check out the address that was on file for Jon Murphy to see if the professor actually was gone for the weekend, or if he was just sending up a smoke screen to hide where he really was.

There were also those two other faceless bodies lying in their morgue whose identities were still a complete mystery. She didn't think that she and her partner would be able to find out who they were, but who knew? Maybe they would get lucky.

Negative thinking never solved anything.

It was a short drive from the precinct to her home. Cheyenne pulled up in front of her garage in a few minutes and decided to park her vehicle at the curb. She was too tired to maneuver her car into the garage, certainly not without nicking it. Besides, this way she could just hop into her car in the morning and take off.

Granted it only shaved a couple of minutes off her departure time, but in her opinion, every little bit helped. Besides, she silently argued with herself, she did have a new partner to set an example for and from what she had gathered, he seemed to like coming in early. It wouldn't do to be shown up by the detective she was in the process of training, she thought, despite the fact that she had gotten him in a completely pretrained mode.

Getting out of her car, Cheyenne hit the button

that locked all four doors simultaneously, then made her way to the front door. She opened it and caught herself wishing that she had a pet dog or cat waiting to greet her.

It wasn't the first time she had entertained this thought. Most of her family had either pets or children, not to mention significant others waiting for them to come home to.

For some reason, the house felt lonelier to her tonight. It undoubtedly had to be all this talk about her uncle's party being thrown Saturday and her family showing up.

She should have gotten more involved in the planning stages, Cheyenne thought. Being busy planning a family get-together would have probably taken the edge off this odd loneliness that seemed to insist on nibbling away at her.

Cheyenne turned on the light as she entered the two-story house. Maybe she needed to get one of those devices that turned the lights on after a certain time, she thought. It wouldn't feel as empty—or as lonely—walking into the house after sundown— and she always came in after sundown, she thought.

Tomorrow, she promised herself as she stepped out of her shoes. She'd think about all this tomorrow. If she didn't get to bed right now, she wasn't going to be good for anything come tomorrow.

With that, Cheyenne stripped off her clothes one piece at a time as she quickly made her way into her bedroom. Tomorrow, if there was any extra time, she was going to look into getting a pet, she promised herself.

Anything except a goldfish.

Cheyenne smiled to herself. After all, she thought, she couldn't very well hug a goldfish.

Chapter 13

Cheyenne got into the office the next morning barely ahead of her partner, which meant that she had gotten in extremely early.

Consequently, the day wound up feeling as if it was at least thirty-six hours long—maybe even longer.

After spending an hour attempting to do further research to ascertain if the woman they were looking into was indeed the mother that Eve Richardson had asked them to find, they decided to temporarily suspend that search until they were able to talk to Professor Murphy face-to-face.

Closing her folder, Cheyenne looked up at her partner.

"Let's see if the bodies in the morgue wind up triggering anything for us or not," Cheyenne told him after an hour of futile searching had gone by.

"Well, you sold me. Doing that is better than going around in circles, getting cross-eyed looking through the files," Jeff agreed.

Cheyenne took her time getting up. As she rose to her feet, she looked at her partner. "I get the feeling that whoever did this is one and the same person." She paused for a second as she searched his face. "How about you?"

Jeff reviewed the points that they had discovered that the victims had in common. "Their fingerprints were rubbed off. The same could be said for the women's facial features. Not exactly something that's usually done in a run-of-the-mill murder. So yes, I think that the same person could very well be behind these slayings."

Though she didn't know him all that well yet, her gut told her that Jefferson wouldn't be saying that if he didn't believe it.

"Nice to know that we're on the same page, Jefferson," she said to her partner.

He nodded. "Still remains to be seen if that page is empty or not," he told Cheyenne.

"You really are a happy-go-lucky person, aren't you?" she asked the man with a touch of sarcasm.

He didn't take offense at her words. Instead, he shrugged and told her, "I have been known to be, at times. It depends on the crime and on what was going down at the time. This crime, however, does not fall in the simple range." He knew she knew that, but he reviewed the reasons he thought that way. "Think of the time it must have taken to rub off not just the fingerprints, but the victim's facial features as well."

"The time and the stomach," Cheyenne pointed out, doing her best not to envision the crime or allow it to get to her. "My guess is that it takes a strong kind of stomach to be able to look at a person and then eliminate every single one of their facial features."

She couldn't help shivering as she considered someone doing that sort of thing.

"If you want my thinking on it," her partner said, "My guess is that sort of gruesome undertaking probably gave the person a great deal of satisfaction. Possibly he felt like he was doling out overdue justice."

"To the person he was killing?" Cheyenne asked, trying to ascertain exactly what her partner was thinking.

"Or to the person who that victim represented," her partner suggested.

"So you think the killer felt he was meting out justice?" Cheyenne asked, intrigued and trying to get to the bottom of what her partner was thinking.

"Did you ever see a little kid getting angry at a toy and beat it up? You know that the toy is an inanimate object that couldn't have done anything to the kid to merit that sort of reaction, but he still beats up on it for some imagined slight or wrongdoing. Well, in a way this is kind of the same thing. The killer feels he's correcting some sort of wrongdoing that he suffered at the hands of the person that the victim obviously represents."

"Which means that we're dealing with a real psychopath," she pointed out.

"Terrific," Jeff murmured with a shake of his head. "If that's the case, we really need to put an end to him."

"If we're right," Cheyenne qualified, "that isn't going to be as easy as you might think," she told him as they got into the elevator. She pressed for the basement, which was where the morgue was located. "First we're going to need to find the person who is killing these women, and in effect, attempting to wipe them off the face of the earth. For that to happen, we're going to need to take baby steps, McDougall. Baby steps," she emphasized as they got out of the elevator.

The medical examiner looked up from what he was doing when the two detectives walked into the man's autopsy room. He was one of several MEs who were on call to perform the autopsies. No one wanted to wear these medical professionals out. It was a rather gruesome business.

"Detective Cavanaugh," the medical examiner said, nodding at her. "And I take it that this is your new partner." He allowed his voice to trail off, waiting for the name to be filled in.

Cheyenne smiled. "Right as usual, Dr. Barlow. This is Detective Jefferson McDougall, fresh from a precinct in Texas," she told the ME. "Jeff, this is one of our medical examiners, Dr. Adrian Barlow."

Barlow, who was shorter than Cheyenne's new partner, nodded as he put his hand out to the new man. "Welcome to Autopsy, Detective McDougall." And then he looked at Cheyenne. "So, how's he working out? Is he filling your old partner's slot?" he asked genially.

"Well, I definitely miss Wade, but yes, he actually is. Rather admirably, I'm happy to report," she told the medical examiner.

Barlow nodded. "Good to hear. So, what can I do for you?" he asked, looking from Cheyenne's partner to the woman herself.

"Have you gotten any closer to finding out any of these women's identities?" Detective Cavanaugh asked the medical examiner.

The ME appeared far from happy. "I wish I could say yes and see that beautiful smile of yours, Detective Cavanaugh, but no, I am no closer to identifying these women now than I was when they were first brought in."

"Why don't we do what we did to try to narrow down that first woman who was brought in? Go through the photos of the women who were reported missing in the last six to nine months and try to match them as best we can to these bodies?" Jefferson suggested.

"The woman's daughter came in to tell us she was missing," Cheyenne reminded him. "We're still not a hundred percent positive that we have the right person. But it is beginning to look that way." She was going to hate having to notify that woman about her mother, if it came to that.

"No reason one of these other women couldn't belong to a relative who's trying to locate them," Jefferson brought up.

The medical examiner nodded in agreement. "I'm no detective, but that suggestion gets my vote," Barlow told Cheyenne.

Cheyenne sighed. "Well, we've got a full day ahead of us and we have to do something. That's as good a way to proceed as any, I suppose." Sometimes she really wished her job was a little easier. "Who knows? We might just get lucky."

Jefferson looked at his partner. "You know, I don't hear any enthusiasm in your voice."

"The enthusiasm materializes when we discover that we're actually on the right path," she answered Jeff. "Dr. Barlow, send me all the photographs that you've taken of these two women, along with any other information you might have, including their height and weight, so we have at least *something* to go on."

"Why don't I take care of making those copies?" Jefferson told his partner. He glanced toward Barlow. "The good doctor here already has his hands full."

Barlow smiled broadly at the suggestion. "I'd say that this new partner of yours is a definite step up from the last partner you had. If you ask me, Wade tended to be on the grumpy-old-man side of things," the medical examiner confided to Jeff. The doctor's words were accompanied with a rather broad wink.

"This will be my pleasure, Doctor," Jefferson told the ME. "If you could give me the photos and point me toward your copy machine," Cheyenne's partner requested, "I will be out of your hair as soon as possible."

The medical examiner reached for the files on a nearby table, turned and handed them to Jefferson. "There you go. I do need these back," the doctor emphasized.

"Don't worry, I just need to make copies. There's not much need for them on the open market, Doc," Jefferson told the older man.

Barlow chuckled. "If there was, I can tell you one thing. I'd be a rich man," the medical examiner quipped.

Jefferson smiled. "We're all shooting for that," Cheyenne's partner told the medical examiner.

"Then I hate to tell you this, but I'm afraid that you are definitely in the wrong profession, McDougall," Cheyenne informed her partner.

Jefferson laughed under his breath as he glanced at her. "You think?"

"Oh, I know," Cheyenne emphasized. "Believe me, I definitely *should* know. All my relatives are in law enforcement or at least in some form of law enforcement. There's not a rich person among us—unless you happen to count being rich in accomplishments."

"I don't know. You can't really buy anything with

accomplishments," Cheyenne's partner told her. "It's not exactly currency."

"No, not outright," Cheyenne agreed. "But you can certainly buy a great deal of goodwill with it."

"I'll keep that in mind if I'm ever in the market for goodwill," Jefferson told her. He saw the smile spreading over Cheyenne's lips and that did manage to get his curiosity up. "What?"

"You'd be surprised," she prophesized. "Stoking goodwill though actions happens more often than you might think."

He shrugged. "If you say so," he said. It was obvious to her that her partner didn't think so.

She grinned at him. "I do—and so will you. Your time to be convinced will come," she told him. "Most likely when you least expect it. Okay," she declared, looking at the collection of papers that he had made copies of after returning the originals to the ME. "Let's see if we can find a match to one of these in our recent photos of missing women."

Holding the photos and copies of the files in his hands, Jefferson gestured toward the exit. "Lead the way, O Fearless Leader," her partner said.

"I'm not fearless," Cheyenne denied. "I just happen to be a wee bit pushy."

Both men smiled at one another over that. But when she looked their way, she saw them holding up their hands in abject denial of what she could see they were actually thinking.

"I wouldn't have said that," the medical examiner protested.

"I certainly wouldn't have," her partner quickly assured her.

"Uh-huh," Cheyenne answered. "You're just worried that I'd sic my brothers on you. Well, you don't have to worry about that," she told them, raising her chin. "I fight my own battles if they're there to be fought," she assured the two men. Having said that, she turned her attention toward her partner. "Shall we go?" Cheyenne asked Jefferson.

He nodded. "Yes, ma'am."

Her eyes narrowed, making him think of a pending storm. "Don't 'ma'am' me, Jefferson. It makes me feel like I'm a hundred years old."

Jefferson collected the photos and the folders concerning the two bodies currently residing in the morgue that he had copied so that he and Cheyenne could pore over them and review.

"Well, you certainly don't look anywhere near that," he told her with a smile. "As a matter of fact, if you don't mind me saying it, you look damn good for someone not even a quarter of that age. Sexy, even," he told her with a wide smile.

"Now you have me thinking that I should be sending you over to the eye doctor," Cheyenne told him.

He shook his head as they left the autopsy area. "No, what you should do is just learn to take a compliment, partner."

"If I felt it was merited, I would," she began.

Jefferson held up his hand, stopping her before she could continue.

"Trust me, Cavanaugh, it is definitely merited. I figure that you've got to own at least one mirror. Otherwise you wouldn't be able to style your hair as well as you do. Am I right?" he asked her, his eyes meeting hers.

She felt a warm shiver going up and down her spine. "Just get on the elevator," she told him, gesturing toward it as she pressed the up arrow.

He smiled at her widely as he inclined his head, lessening the space between them. "With pleasure."

Cheyenne murmured something under her breath, but he figured he was better off not asking her to repeat it.

Chapter 14

Cheyenne didn't see it coming until just before it was time to call it a day and finally go home. Even then, she had almost missed it.

"McDougall, come look at this," Cheyenne called to her partner.

Jefferson got up and made his way around her desk and over to her. When he was standing behind her, Cheyenne pointed to a photograph of one of the recently dug-up victims who was presently lying in Autopsy. Cheyenne had the photograph on her desk.

"What does this look like to you?" she asked her partner.

About to go home, Jefferson came up behind her and looked at the area on the photograph she was pointing to. The photograph was of one of the two women who had been discovered buried in the forest and brought in a couple of weeks ago.

"Like something my mother would have definitely punished me for having in my possession as a kid," Jefferson admitted honestly.

Cheyenne nodded. "Good woman, your mother," she commented. "No little boy should be looking at pictures like that. But I'm talking about the victim's left wrist, not the rest of her." She tapped the specific area that she was referring to.

The detective leaned in closer to get a better look at the area being discussed. "Looks to me like some small animal decided to snack on the victim."

"Not entirely. The hungry little critter didn't get it all," she told her partner. "Look closer," she instructed Jefferson. "What do you see?"

Cheyenne caught a little whiff of her partner's aftershave lotion as he bent in over the photograph. It was a slightly heady scent.

The man did smell good, Cheyenne couldn't help thinking. For just a second, she felt aroused, then quickly locked away that feeling. This was neither the time nor the place for that sort of indulgence, she told herself.

He turned toward Cheyenne. Their faces were rather close to one another, Jefferson couldn't help thinking. He looked at the victim's left wrist again. "Is that part of a rose tattoo?" he asked his partner.

"That's what I saw, too," she told him. "Now we have at least part of a description to feed into the computer and look for." And *at least part* was better than nothing, she thought. "People have been caught from far less to go on," she told Jefferson.

"*If* that *is* part of a rose tattoo," Jeff said, squinting as he attempted to study the lower part of the dead woman's left wrist.

"My suggestion is that we make another copy of the photograph. We can each carry a copy with us. That way we can sleep on it and take another look at the tattoo in the morning."

"You mean at your uncle's party?" Jefferson asked, slightly bewildered.

"You know, ordinarily I'd say that isn't such a bad idea," she told her partner as they walked out of the room and into the elevator. "My family members tend to solve crimes together if something really stumps one of us," she told her partner. "But this *is* Uncle Andrew's birthday party and I don't want anything taking away from that, even though I know that Uncle Andrew really wouldn't mind. I know for a fact that he misses being mentally challenged by cases, but I don't think Aunt Rose would take kindly to us bringing 'work' to the party." Cheyenne smiled at the thought. "As it is, she's going to have all she can handle just keeping Uncle Andrew out of the kitchen and not attempting to cook anything."

"Cooking?" Jefferson questioned. Cooking for him meant putting a frozen meal into the microwave, pushing a few buttons and waiting for the prepackaged meal to be done.

Cheyenne nodded as she began to pack up her things for the day. "Yes. Uncle Andrew loves to cook. Cooking at a local restaurant was how Uncle Andrew put himself through school back in the day. And when circumstances necessitated his retiring early as the police chief from the force in order to take care of his five kids when his wife disappeared, he supported his family by going back to cooking."

"His wife disappeared," Jefferson repeated, somewhat bewildered. "Then your aunt Rose wasn't his first wife?" he asked, doing his best to understand and keep the family dynamics straight in his mind.

"Oh, she was. And is," Cheyenne told her partner as they walked out to the elevator.

He looked at her, really confused now. "Let me get this straight. She was lost, causing him to retire. And then she just suddenly turned up? Now I'm really lost."

"The answer is rather simple. Uncle Andrew and Aunt Rose never argued, but they did that night. Aunt Rose drove off in order to cool off. The area was having one of its really rare rainstorms and Aunt Rose wound up driving off the road and into the lake. Her car was found there the next morning, floating in the water. Empty.

"Uncle Andrew hired all sorts of people to search for her, but they didn't find anything. However, he never gave up," Cheyenne told her partner.

"Thirteen years later, while following a lead on a case upstate, Uncle Andrew's youngest daughter, Rayne, ran into a waitress at a diner that she thought looked a great deal like a photograph of Aunt Rose that she carried around in her wallet." Cheyenne pressed the down button to the elevator. "When Rayne went home, she immediately told her father about the waitress. Uncle Andrew lost no time in driving up to the diner to see for himself and check the woman out.

"Long story short—" Cheyenne said.

"Too late," Jefferson told her as they got off the elevator. "But please, continue."

Cheyenne gave her partner a look, then told him, "The waitress turned out to be Aunt Rose. The experience of plunging into the lake in her car was such a shock, it caused her to get amnesia. Uncle Andrew turning up at the diner, telling her the story about how they wound up being separated and then taking her back home with him eventually wound up jarring Aunt Rose's memory.

"I'm told," Cheyenne concluded, "that Aunt Rose hasn't taken a moment for granted since she came back to the land of the living when the whole story that Uncle Andrew told her finally sank in."

Standing at the outer door, ready to leave, Jefferson looked at his partner and whistled softly under his breath. "Wow."

"I guess that sums it up rather nicely," Cheyenne admitted with a wide smile.

"Makes my life seem really dull and boring in comparison," Jefferson answered.

"I certainly wouldn't call it dull and boring. You were in the Marines and when you completed your tour of duty, you joined the police department in El Paso, Texas. That hardly seems dull and boring to me," she pointed out to her partner.

"It all depends on where your focus is. Searching for a missing wife for thirteen years certainly requires a great deal of dedication and patience," he said with conviction.

"Tell you what," Cheyenne said brightly, one hand on the door, about to push it open. "This will definitely give you something to talk about with my aunt and uncle tomorrow."

Her comment caught him off guard. "Is that still on?" he asked.

"Why shouldn't it be?" she questioned. "Uncle Andrew's birthday hasn't changed dates and my aunt Rose is still throwing him the biggest party she can. Everyone is planning on coming—and 'everyone' includes you. Remember, Uncle Andrew is looking forward to meeting you, both as my uncle and as the former chief of the Aurora Police Department," Cheyenne said.

"What if I don't measure up in your uncle's opinion?" Jefferson asked Cheyenne.

"Only way that could possibly happen is if you turn out to be the serial killer we're looking for," she told the man. "You're not, are you?" she asked, tongue-in-cheek.

"Nope," he answered, shaking his head from side to side in denial.

"So you're fine," Cheyenne assured him. "I will be around to either pick you up at one o'clock, or have you follow me in your car to my uncle's house around that time. Your choice."

"You don't have to do that," he told her.

"I didn't say I *had* to," she pointed out. "I thought I made it clear that I *wanted* to. So, is one o'clock all right with you, or do you want to go earlier?"

"One o'clock is fine. I know I asked before, but I don't remember what you answered. Should I bring anything?" Jefferson asked her.

"And I told you just bring yourself and that'll be more than enough. If you really want to bring something…" Cheyenne began.

"Yes?" he asked, prodding eagerly.

"Bring a card," she told him.

He looked at her in disappointment and all but rolled his eyes. "That hardly seems like anything."

"A *nice* card," she underscored.

Jefferson sighed. Cheyenne was definitely not helping. "What's your uncle's favorite wine or alcoholic beverage?"

"Oh no, don't go that route. My other uncles and cousins will definitely inundate Uncle Andrew with enough alcohol to practically drown the man," she assured her partner. "It's very hard shopping for someone who says he doesn't want anything except for his family to be happy and well fed."

"I can see how that might be frustrating," Jefferson agreed.

"Just come and have a good time. That's guaranteed to make the man happy. Trust me," Cheyenne told her partner.

"You really are a selfless bunch of people, aren't you?" Jefferson asked, shaking his head in disbelief.

"That's what I've been trying to tell you," Cheyenne said. "Okay, I'll be by your apartment in the morning."

"I thought you said you'd be there at one," he said.

"What I meant is that we'll be at Uncle Andrew's at one, and since I never learned Dorothy's trick of clicking my heels together to instantly be transported to my destination, I'm going to have to be at your place before one o'clock."

"Dorothy?" he questioned, confused.

She looked at him to see if he was on the level. "Dorothy Gale. The heroine in *The Wizard of Oz*," she prompted, then said in disbelief, "You're kidding, right? Didn't you ever watch it on TV?"

"Sorry, I didn't have a traditional childhood. My mother didn't believe in wasting time with cartoons."

"*The Wizard of Oz* wasn't a cartoon, at least not in the beginning. It was a classic story written for children. I can see that there are a lot of gaps in your education. It'll give us something to talk about during those long stakeouts," she told him. "But right now, we need to hit the road in order to get some sleep. Okay, let's get going, partner."

"Right behind you," Jefferson told her as they walked toward the parking lot.

Cheyenne caught herself smiling. She found that she was enjoying being with Jefferson more and more with each passing day. The situation was becoming promising.

Chapter 15

It was a shame that she couldn't sleep in, given that this wasn't a workday and that for once, there weren't any emergency calls from the precinct sending her to the scene of some crime or other, or even anything remotely close to that. In all honesty, Cheyenne sincerely doubted that there would be, given that everyone knew that this was the former chief of police's birthday and close family members were all planning on being at the gathering, celebrating the occasion.

Of course there were patrolmen and women on duty, but in addition to that Aurora had never been exactly known for being the hub of any real ongoing crime wave, or anything even remotely like that.

But the moment she opened her eyes, Cheyenne

threw off her covers and was on her feet, making her way into the bathroom for a quick, bracing shower.

She was in and out, showered and dried in less than ten minutes.

Not exactly her personal best, she thought, but it would definitely do. Cheyenne wanted to get going as soon as humanly possible.

She dried her long blond hair and carefully put it up in the style she knew her uncle favored seeing on her. Finished arranging her hair, Cheyenne slipped into a soft, silky aqua dress that flirted with the tops of her knees and lovingly hugged her curves. After dealing with the ugliness she sometimes came in contact with on the job, Cheyenne savored the gentler, nicer moments that came her way. Her uncle's birthday definitely fell under that heading.

Once she finished putting on her makeup, Cheyenne critically surveyed the results from all angles. With a nod of her head, she decided that for once, she was satisfied.

She slipped on her high heels, grabbed her purse from the side table where she had dropped it the night before, and checked to make sure she had her car keys with her. She picked up the beautiful card she had chosen expressly for her uncle and then made her way to her front door.

Cheyenne caught her reflection in the mirror by the door and looked herself over one last time.

"Look out, Detective Jefferson McDougall—prepare to have your socks melted right off your feet," she murmured to the man who wasn't there.

With that, Cheyenne made her way out the front door, then paused to lock it. She tried the lock to make sure that it took and couldn't accidentally be opened.

This was a safe house within a very safe neighborhood that was domiciled in a very safe city, she thought, but she had learned that it never paid to be cocky when it came to personal safety. Taking the extra precaution was always a good thing because fate was always waiting to prove you wrong and cause things to wind up caving in on themselves.

She had learned a long time ago that if anything could go wrong, it definitely would.

It was a jaded way to approach things, but she knew that it was far from wrong.

Once in her car, it took her a moment to recall the address where her new partner was staying. When she did, she turned the ignition on, moved her foot off the brake and took off.

Jefferson lived less than fifteen minutes away from her own home, which in turn wasn't all that far away from where the police precinct was located. She liked that, liked being that close to work. From her point of view, it made things a great deal simpler.

It was an exceptionally nice neighborhood, she thought, taking the area in as she drove through it. She was familiar with every inch of Aurora in one form or another. The city itself had been built up in stages. This particular part of the development had been erected at a later time, after the university and hospital had been built.

Initially, there were only a handful of schools and shopping centers put into the area. Eventually things developed further and yet, remarkably, Aurora never had that crowded, overdone look to it, she marveled. From a very young age, when things like this began to sink in, Cheyenne found herself never wanting to live anywhere else but right here in Aurora.

She couldn't help wondering what her partner thought of it, coming from Texas the way he had.

That was why she had joined the rest of her family in law enforcement. She wanted to keep her city peaceful and orderly, free of any wrongdoers—like the serial killer she suspected was currently haunting Aurora's streets. She was itching to bring that man's reign of terror to an end, and quickly.

"No, no shop talk," she told herself out loud. "Today is all about Uncle Andrew. Time enough to find and end this hateful man tomorrow."

She turned down a side street, following it to the next light, then into a residential development that was across from an area that contained four movie theaters.

Cheyenne thought that she hadn't been in one of those for a long time. There never seemed to be enough time for that, she realized. Any free time she actually managed to find she used to just kick back and relax—or at least tried to, she thought.

After parking her vehicle down the block, she got

out and made her way to the address she had input into her cell phone.

"124 Hamilton Street," she murmured to herself as she read it out loud. "This must be the place," she said in a comedic voice. Bracing herself, Cheyenne rang the doorbell. Within seconds, the front door swung open.

Jefferson was in the doorway, about to say something, but then the words seemed to just dry up on his lips, never managing to emerge as his mouth dropped open.

"Something wrong?" she asked him, not sure just how to interpret the look on her partner's face.

His eyes washed over her. It was obvious that he was enjoying what he was seeing. "No, not a thing," he told her with simple honesty.

"You're staring," she pointed out.

The look in his eyes was smiling at her. "I know," Jefferson acknowledged. "You clean up really well, Cavanaugh," he told her with a broad smile.

"Thank you. I wasn't aware that I needed cleaning up," she told him drolly.

"You don't, which is what makes looking at you this way such a fantastic pleasure," he informed his partner.

"I had no idea that you could lay it on so thickly," she said.

He merely grinned at her, his eyes washing over her again. "I guess there are a lot of things about me that you don't know yet," he said.

"I guess not. That's what working together is for, I

suppose. So we can learn about one another," Cheyenne told the man. "Not that you having that look on your face doesn't do a lot for my ego, but if you don't want one of my brothers taking you aside for 'a talk,' maybe you should find a way to table that expression for a while."

"I wasn't aware that I was looking at you in any particular way," Jefferson told her, doing his best to disguise the look on his face.

"You were," she said, reaching her vehicle as she smiled at him. "And if you really weren't aware of it, then maybe you're not as good a detective as I thought you were."

The detective's smile only broadened. "There's a reason behind everything. I'd hold off making a judgment if I were you."

She nodded. "No problem." She paused to look at him. "Now, do you want to follow me to the party, or would you prefer that I do the driving to my uncle's place?"

Jeff laughed under his breath. "I know my father would have hated to hear me saying this, but since you're familiar with wherever it is that we're going, why don't you just do the driving to the chief's house?" her partner suggested to her.

"You don't strike me as the type to raise your hands and just back away from something like driving a vehicle. You mind if I ask you why?" Cheyenne asked.

"It's very simple. I don't want to risk arriving at your uncle's place uptight," he said honestly. "Facing your entire family is enough of an uptight situation. Not to mention that the chief of detectives and the head of CSI are going to be there as well. That, in my opinion, is definitely facing a full plate. Actually, more than a full plate."

Cheyenne inclined her head and then nodded in response. "I can definitely accept that," Cheyenne told her partner.

He smiled at her. "Glad we're in agreement."

She started her car and put it in gear. "Ready?" she asked him whimsically as she pulled her car away from the curb.

Her question amused him. "If I said 'no,' would you pull over?"

"No," she answered, on the road. "I would however ask you why you suddenly changed your mind."

"I suppose that the best answer to that is that I'm a little worried about putting my best foot forward," he admitted.

"Don't be," she told him. "You got along well with the brothers you did meet at the bar that first day. The same goes for the cousins you met there." She glanced in his direction. "Maybe I shouldn't say this, but in my opinion, you seem to get along very well with just about anyone you meet or interact with," Cheyenne told him.

"Thank you. But why shouldn't you say it?" he asked. "It's not like I'm about to get a swelled head or lord it over anyone."

She spared him a quick look from the corner of her

eye. "No, I don't believe that you would. And you'll find that my entire family is incredibly easy to get along with."

Jefferson nodded his head. He was allowing this to mean too much to him, he thought. "Okay," her partner said, squaring his shoulders, "I'm ready to meet them."

"Good," she responded, adding, "because we're almost there."

She turned down the next street, then drove about half a block farther. That took her past a local inner park. By the time she reached the end of that, she stopped at a large two-story house that seemed to go on forever in both directions.

"Okay, Jefferson, we're here," Cheyenne finally announced.

Jeff's eyes grew huge as he looked at the house. "This? This is your uncle Andrew's house?"

"This is Uncle Andrew's house," Cheyenne acknowledged.

"It's huge," his partner declared as she drove past the building.

"Aren't we going in?" Jeff asked. "You just went by it."

"I know. Parking is going to be really tricky. I'm going to leave this car on the other side of the park," she explained. "There are a lot of people who're going to be coming to Uncle Andrew's house. We have to leave some space for them."

He thought that was being exceedingly thoughtful

of her, but he was beginning to see that that was her way. "This is some house," he commented, turning in his seat to get a better look at it.

"Uncle Andrew bought this house almost forty-five years ago," she told her partner. "Houses in Aurora were going for a song back then. Now it's a song, a dance and a lot of other things thrown in as well," she told him, her mouth curving. "Those early houses were a real bargain back then."

Cheyenne stopped her car and then pulled up the handbrake. "Ready?" she asked with a smile.

"Lead the way," her partner told her, gesturing beyond her vehicle.

She got out, rounded the hood and then waited for Jefferson to join her. When he did, they walked back to the house together.

"Remember," she coached, "My uncle is a very kind man. They are all very kind men—and women," she emphasized, watching her partner's expression. "And you are going to look back on today as the beginning of a brand-new life," she promised.

Jefferson had his doubts about that, but he wasn't about to argue with her, definitely not right before they walked into the house.

Later would take care of itself, he thought as he watched her open the front door and walk in.

Squaring his shoulders, Jefferson followed his partner inside.

Chapter 16

Andrew Cavanaugh did not look overly happy when Cheyenne and her new partner walked into the former chief of police's house. But it had nothing to do with them, or with the other dozen or so people who had arrived early to pay honor to the much-loved patriarch.

"She's banning me from my own kitchen," Cheyenne's uncle Andrew complained with feeling as he waved his hand in his wife's general direction. He couldn't remember a time when he had not been allowed into his own kitchen—*ever*.

Rose overheard him and raised her voice. "You are not supposed to be cooking for yourself, not to mention for a whole bunch of other people who are going to be here on your own birthday, Andrew,"

Rose told her husband. She turned toward Cheyenne. "Tell him he can't, please, Cheyenne."

There was sympathy in the young woman's eyes for both her uncle and her aunt. She sided with both of them for different reasons.

"He knows that, Aunt Rose." Cheyenne turned toward her uncle. "It's just that his cooking is really quite exceptional."

Feeling vindicated, Andrew smiled his thanks at his niece. But that thanks turned out to be short-lived.

"Even so," Cheyenne continued pointedly, "you have to allow people to do things for you, Uncle Andrew. Look at it this way, it makes them feel as good to do that as you feel when you're cooking for them."

Andrew raised his eyebrow. "She has the makings of a real negotiator, this one," the chief commented to Jefferson, nodding at Cheyenne. And then he looked more closely at the young detective. "I take it that you're the new partner I've heard so much about."

Jeff instantly put out his hand to her uncle Andrew, happy to officially meet the man. "Yes, sir. I'm Jefferson McDougall," he said, introducing himself.

Andrew inclined his head, making it seem that he was listening closely to the young man. "You're the one who came here from Texas, am I right?"

"Yes, sir. By way of the El Paso Police Department," Jeff said, quickly elaborating.

"McDougall was a Marine before he joined the

police department," Cheyenne told her uncle. She knew her uncle would be interested in that as well.

Andrew nodded. "All very good character-building experiences," the former police chief declared with approval. After a beat, the chief realized that he was hogging the spotlight. That just wasn't his way. "Well, come in, come in. Join the party," he urged, gesturing toward the large living room that was already beginning to become rather crowded. "Cheyenne can do the honors when it comes to the introductions."

"You can come join us," Cheyenne told her uncle, adding, "since you're not cooking or baking anything for once."

Andrew glanced over his shoulder in his wife's direction, a touch of concern etched into his face. "I think that I should hang around, staying close by," he explained to the two detectives who had just arrived. "You know, just in case Rose decides that maybe she actually *does* need me."

"I heard that," Rose said, raising her voice so that she could to be heard across the kitchen. She crossed over to where her husband and they others were standing. "Don't get me wrong, Andrew. I worship the ground you walk on, I always have. But I really *can* handle this."

"No one is saying that you can't handle it, dear," Andrew told his wife. "I just want to hang around so I can pretend to feel useful. You wouldn't want to deny me that on my birthday, would you?"

Rose laughed as she shook her head, then looked in Cheyenne and her partner's direction. "Who would have ever thought that my husband could actually be such a manipulator?"

Rather than be offended, Andrew laughed as he wrapped one arm around his wife's shoulders and hugged her to him. "You flatter me."

Rose laughed. "Hardly." She turned toward Cheyenne and the young detective with her. "Go. Mingle. Introduce this nice young man around. I promise I will call for help if it turns out that I need you."

The latter bent forward and brushed her lips against her uncle Andrew's cheek. "Remember to behave," Cheyenne teased him.

Turning toward her partner, she hooked her arm through Jeff's, drawing him into the large living room. "In case you missed it, that's our cue to go and mingle."

Beginning to leave the entrance, Jeff regarded his hostess and asked, "Do you need any help? I'm not much of a cook, but if you need anything else done, like potatoes peeled, glasses put out, beverages poured..." The detective's voice trailed off, letting the woman fill in the blank spaces the way she saw fit.

"Well, aren't you sweet?" Aunt Rose enthused. "But no," she replied, waving the duo on their way into the living room. "Everything is under control. You two just go on out and mingle. Introduce your partner to anyone who might not have met him yet,

Cheyenne, you can guess how confusing it is when you're the new kid on the block."

Cheyenne nodded.

"I can vividly sympathize with that feeling," she replied even though she had never experienced it herself. She looked at Jeff. "C'mon, 'new kid,' let's start getting you circulated."

Jeff allowed himself to be led off to join the cluster of family members gathered in the next room.

"Your aunt seems really nice," Jefferson told Cheyenne.

"I'd say that all my relatives are," Cheyenne said to her partner. "I told you that when you said yes to my invitation."

"Yes, you did," Jeff agreed. "But I didn't think you really meant it. That's something almost everyone says about their family to a stranger who they are inviting over for the first time."

Cheyenne fixed him with a look that was meant to put him in his place. She didn't like being lumped in with other people in this sort of fashion.

"I never say anything that I don't mean," she informed her partner.

"That would make you a very unique woman," he informed Cheyenne.

"What's that supposed to mean?" she asked him. "Are you trying to say that all women lie?"

"No, I didn't mean that they did it outright," he told her quickly, then added, "They just bend the truth once in a while."

"Well, I don't," she informed her skeptical partner sharply. "I'm a firm believer in either telling the truth, or saying nothing at all. Now, can we table this please, until we're not surrounded by members of my family?"

He was more than willing to leave the subject. "Sure, we can get back to this at a later date," Jeff told his partner genially. "Any time that you want to."

"Good," Cheyenne responded with a nod of her head. "Now, put your happy face on. I've got a whole bunch of cousins to introduce you to."

Jefferson glanced in her direction. "Is there going to be some sort of a quiz at the end of the evening?"

It wasn't easy, but Cheyenne found that she managed to maintain a straight face as she answered, "Yes," in confirmation. "You won't be able to leave my uncle's house and go home unless you are able to score at least eighty out of a hundred."

Jeff suddenly stopped moving and just stared at her. "You're kidding."

Cheyenne had a hard time answering his question without laughing out loud. "Yes, I'm kidding. Did your sense of humor get completely erased when you walked into my uncle's house ?"

Her partner frowned. "No. It's just that you seem to be able to deadpan incredibly well."

"Next time I'll try to remember to snicker in between statements," Cheyenne promised, her mouth curving.

It was Jeff's turn to maintain a straight face while

answering. "Yes, I can see how that might be helpful."

"So, you do have a sense of humor," she said as if that was some sort of a huge revelation in itself. The corners of her mouth curved as her eyes sparkled.

"Yeah, every once in a while, if I dig deep enough, I can actually find it," Jefferson told said.

Cheyenne nodded her head in approval. "Well, I suggest that you keep on digging. It definitely helps move the situation along," she told him with a warm smile. "Since the line of work we're involved in can be extremely grim, it really helps to have a sense of humor within reach. Otherwise what we do for a living and the people we come in contact with can wind up sucking every bit of joy right out of you and just leave you completely dry and empty on the inside."

Replaying her own words in her head, Cheyenne blew out a breath. "You know, I think that Uncle Andrew's birthday arrived just in time to make me feel better. Nothing like mingling with people you love to keep your mind moving on the straight and narrow."

"What if you didn't have any people you love?" Jefferson asked her.

She had a feeling that her partner was talking about himself. She could feel her heart going out to him. "Tell you what, I'll lend you some of mine," she told him, flashing a warm smile in her partner's direction. "No charge. As a matter of fact, I can start right now. Come meet my cousins, Dugan, Morgan and Sully," Cheyenne told him as she drew her partner over to the three men she had mentioned. All three looked very similar to each other.

But then, truthfully, Jeff had begun to feel that all the Cavanaughs, at least those who were related to one another by blood, seemed to have exceedingly similar features.

Cheyenne could almost tell what her partner was thinking. "They're my uncle Angus's sons," she said.

Jeff was beginning to feel rather lost as more and more names came flying in his direction. Nodding and smiling at the three men she had just introduced to him, he felt honor-bound to admit his confusion.

"Which is which?" he asked and then went on to say, "You know, this whole thing might be easier if you just wore name badges at this gathering. At least in the beginning when you have someone new attending," he told the group of cousins she had just brought him over to.

"There's no penalty for getting anyone's name wrong," Dugan, the tallest of the threesome, told Jefferson. "We know this has to be pretty confusing to someone new to the group."

"See, I told you they were nice," Cheyenne told her partner. "Besides, there's only one of you they have to meet, while you have a huge slew of relatives to attempt to keep straight. It definitely does get easier over time, but it's definitely not an immediate process."

"I guess I can live with that," Jeff murmured more to himself than to Cheyenne.

"That's the spirit," another cousin said, catching Jefferson's statement as he joined the group. He clapped Cheyenne's partner on the back. "Hi, I'm Murdoch," he told Jeff, shaking his hand.

"Murdoch," Jeff repeated. He caught himself thinking that it wasn't exactly a common name, at least to the best of his knowledge. "Hello," he said, doing his best to commit the man's face and name to memory.

Murdoch turned toward Cheyenne, taking her in as well. "I hear you two might have a cold case involving a serial killer on your hands," he said to his cousin. He looked extremely interested.

"Word does seem to get around," was Cheyenne's only comment on Murdoch's words.

But Murdoch was not about to drop the subject just yet. "How's that coming along?" he asked.

"Slowly," Cheyenne answered honestly. "Very slowly." She definitely was not happy about the pace. "Why do you ask? Surely you've got enough cases of your own to keep you busy," she told her cousin.

"Oh, I do, I do," he assured his cousin and her partner. "Except that now I think I might have a case on my hands that just might tie in with yours. Or at least might be connected to your killer."

Jeff's ears instantly perked up at that. "Send the evidence over on Monday morning," he told the other man. "But as intriguing as all this sounds, I think your aunt Rose might be upset if she finds us talking about serial killers—or police business in general—here today."

Dugan nodded, placing an arm around both Cheyenne's and Jeff's shoulders. "The new guy is right, little cousin. As interesting as this case might be, we don't want Aunt Rose getting wind of this."

"I don't find it interesting," Cheyenne informed Dugan. "I just want to stop this horrid person cold in his tracks."

"So do we," Dugan agreed. "But Uncle Andrew only has one birthday to celebrate. So let's celebrate it."

"Amen to that. So any of you catch that new mystery series that was on last night?" Morgan asked, deftly switching subjects.

He slowly looked at the faces of his brothers and cousins who were currently gathered together in a corner of the room. In his opinion, the program was basically a safe enough topic for him to be able to broach and talk about at the moment.

Chapter 17

His face turned ugly as he glared at the woman lying in a heap on the forest ground. "You shouldn't have scratched me, you bitch," he growled, running his hand over the fresh marks on his face.

Glancing down at his hand, he saw that there was blood on it.

That bitch had drawn blood! He fairly fumed.

The anger he felt increased tenfold. He could all but feel it flaring in his veins. If he hadn't already killed the woman, he would have done it right this minute. She certainly deserved it.

No loss, the instructor told himself. Lauren Dixon had thought of herself as a scholar.

A *scholar* of all things, he sneered.

The pathetic old woman should have been exceedingly grateful that he'd even allowed her to sit in on his lectures, much less looked at and graded the paper she'd handed in.

In his opinion, he had been generous, giving her a Sixty-five. If he had been honest, it would have been less than that. Much less than that. And then she had had the unmitigated gall to actually argue with him about it, telling him he wasn't being fair. That she deserved a better grade than that.

Deserved, of all things, he thought bitterly. He'd show her *deserved*, Murphy thought as he dragged the woman's freshly wrapped and covered body through the woods.

Because the old bat reminded him of his aunt Lily, he thought it only fitting that he bury her in the same area where he had once disposed of his aunt—though there wasn't a drop of oxygen left in Lauren Dixon's lungs the way there had been in Aunt Lily's when he'd buried her.

Oh well, Murphy thought philosophically, he supposed he couldn't have everything.

But he could still hope, he told himself.

Hope.

The hallmark of little men and women. His mother had taught him that just before she had finally taken off, he recalled. It was a lesson that had stuck with him over the years.

The expression on his face turned even uglier than it already had been. Memories of his aunt always did that to him, he thought. The hunger for revenge had been growing and eating away at him for several days now, but he really had had no intention of killing this old grandmother to alleviate the pain.

Old grandmother, he mocked to himself. The old crone had made sure everyone knew that about her, like it was some sort of a badge of honor. Like every stray dog or cat couldn't have a litter at the drop of a hat.

The true accomplishment was to make the litter feel as if they were wanted.

Fresh anger creased Murphy's brow as he threw dirt on top of the wrapped body, intending to bury it from view. He needed to get a grip on himself. As good as it felt, choking the life out of these old biddies, he couldn't allow himself to get carried away like that.

Suspicions would be aroused and he could certainly do without that.

Murphy moved a little faster. He needed to bury the old crow's body before the sun began coming up.

He blamed the old bat for the growing ache in his shoulders.

She had forced him to do this, he thought angrily, damning her in his heart.

"It's really getting late," Jefferson noted, glancing at the watch on his left wrist.

He and Cheyenne were still at the former chief of police's house. Only a little less than half the guests had left the party so far. It was very obvious that no one really wanted to leave. They were having much too good a time.

"I never took you for Cinderella," Cheyenne commented, looking at her partner. "Is this really too late for you?"

She had gotten the distinct impression that he was the type who could stay up, partying all night long when the whim hit him.

"No, I just thought that a lot of these people probably have to be on call tomorrow," her partner said, sipping from his glass as he surveyed all the faces that were surrounding them.

"Trust me, if they have to be on call and alert, they will be," she assured him. "This bunch doesn't let work slide. Neither would they let a good time slide if that came up," she added, telling him, "You'll find that out after being in Aurora for a while."

Her partner shrugged in response to her comment. "Uh-huh."

"This was a really wonderful dinner, Aunt Rose," Cheyenne told her aunt almost an hour later, adding her voice to those of many of the people who were preparing to leave the party.

Rose flashed a smile at her niece, obviously grateful for the kind words. "Granted it wasn't as good as it could have been if Andrew had done the cooking, but at least I had the satisfaction of seeing my husband sit back and allow himself to be served." She leaned into Andrew, stood on her toes and affectionately ruffled his full head of gray-streaked hair.

"It wasn't that bad, being served, right, honey?" she asked pointedly.

Andrew sighed deeply at her question. "Whatever you say, darling," he answered her. He looked around at the guests who were closest to him. "What do you say? Are you guys about ready for another round of drinks?"

"Much as we'd love to toast you again," Brian told his older brother, "I think if we indulged in another round—or twelve as is your habit—you and Seamus are going to have to wind up pouring us and the rest of this crowd into our cars," the chief of d's said.

"Well, you're all welcome to sleep here if you need to," Rose said warmly to the family members who had not cleared out of the big house yet.

"I know it's a big house," Brian told his sister-in-law, "but having the rest of us stay here is really asking for trouble, even if you could actually stuff the rest of us all in here."

And he should know, Brian thought. He had watched as his family members had grown in number over the years, from a small cluster of people until the resulting mass of members seemed to become almost insurmountable. Incalculable.

"Well then," Rose asked whimsically, looking around at her guests, "do you want me to start singing 'The Party's Over' as I hold the front door open for you?"

Andrew laughed as he hugged his wife to him. "Nothing subtle about my little wife here," he couldn't help commenting with a chuckle. "Seriously, maybe you all should start heading home before you run the risk of falling asleep behind the wheel. I don't want any of you to risk getting into an accident on my account—or even not on my account."

Brian laughed as he shook his head. "That's my big brother for you, always thinking about making sure that we're all safe."

"Well, it's a lot better than thinking about work. We all deserve to take a break from that once in a while," Sean said, adding his voice to that of his brothers.

"Amen to that," Seamus said, agreeing whole-heartedly with his sons' sentiments. Even at his age, he definitely enjoyed partying with his family.

It had been years since Seamus Cavanaugh had been an active member of law enforcement, but that didn't mean that he had lost all interest in the matter. The cases that the law enforcement officers— even those who were not part of his family—were involved in still really managed to pique his interest and he followed them whenever he could.

"All right, so if you're not staying here," Andrew told his guests and relatives, "like I said, it's time for all of you to hit the road and go home—slowly," the former chief of police told his family and guests. "And I want to thank you all for coming," he said in all sincerity.

A lot of voices chimed in, echoing what a great time they'd all had and how much they were looking forward to the next gathering Andrew was going to have. Everyone knew that it would be soon.

Family and friends left the former chief of police's home. Every one of them was beaming.

People were funneling out through the front door, looking somewhat sleepy but extremely satisfied with what had gone down.

Jeff was directly beside Cheyenne. A misstep had her suddenly slipping and stumbling.

Instantly alert, her partner made a grab for her arm, wrapping his own arm around her to steady her before she wound up falling.

It was hard to say which of them was more surprised, Cheyenne or Jefferson. Jeff was afraid that she might wind up being resentful over his reaction, but instead, Cheyenne beamed at him and wound up squeezing his hand.

"Thank you," she told him as they made their way to the curb. They were going toward where she had parked her car hours earlier. The area didn't appear to be nearly as crowded as it had been when they had arrived and most likely not nearly as crowded as it had become when the cars were parked here for the height of the event.

"Well, at least I won't have to fight traffic in order to get out of the area," she told Jeff as they came up to her vehicle.

Pointing her keys at her car, Cheyenne hit the single button on her key fob. That caused all four of the locks on her car to pop open simultaneously, sounding not unlike soldiers standing at attention and shooting their guns at the same time.

Glancing over the roof of her vehicle, she told Jeff, "Go on, get in."

He frowned slightly. "You know, it just doesn't seem right, you driving me home. I should be the one driving you."

"That's okay. Next time, I'll let you drive me home," Cheyenne told him. "That's what working at the precinct in Aurora is all about, Jeff. People looking out for one another. Being nice to one another."

He heard what wasn't being said. "So there's going to be a next time?"

"Of course there will be a next time." How could he even doubt that? "Now that you've gotten your feet wet, gatherings at Uncle Andrew's are going to be a recurring part of life for you."

Jefferson had to admit that he was surprised. At his last job, at the precinct in El Paso, the people he worked with would always go home at the end of the day and, other than getting together for the occasional drink at the local bar, they wouldn't see one another until the following morning.

"Seeing each other at work isn't enough?" Jefferson questioned Cheyenne.

She laughed. She supposed her partner had a point, but it definitely was not *her* point. "Seeing each other at work is only the beginning."

They made their way down the quiet, darkened streets, heading toward the apartment that Jeff was renting. "So," Cheyenne asked him pointedly, "what do you think?"

Jefferson wasn't quite sure exactly what she was asking him. "You're going to have to be a little clearer than that with your question, Cavanaugh. What do I think about what?" he asked. "Are you asking about the food, the company, the…" His voice trailed off, letting Cheyenne fill in the blank any way that she saw fit.

"That's easy," she answered him. "I'm asking about all of it. Knowing you, I expect you probably have an opinion about everything." She saw his building directly up ahead. "You strike me as someone who forms opinions on a great many subjects as he goes along."

Finally reaching the apartment building, Cheyenne pulled up in front of it. Turning off the engine, she pivoted toward Jefferson and waited for him to answer her question.

"Well, you were right," her partner admitted. "I did have a really great time. Even better than I actually thought I would. Your uncles and aunts and all the rest of your family and friends went out of their way to make not just me comfortable, but everyone else who was there as well," he told his partner. "I honestly didn't think that could happen, given that I didn't actually know any of them before this party. But I really have to give them credit—all of them," he emphasized, smiling at Cheyenne. "By the middle of the evening, I felt as if I had known them not just for a few hours, or even that whole day, but really for a very long time. I think that's a gift," he admitted. And then his eyes washed over her. "The same sort of gift that you have." Jeff smiled to himself. "I think that I did a really good thing, coming out here to Aurora."

"Why did you come out here?" she asked, curious as to what his motivation had been.

"Someone actually told me about Aurora in passing," he admitted. "My dad had died. I didn't have any real family ties to where I was living, so I thought I'd give Aurora it a shot."

The story moved her. Turning toward him, Cheyenne smiled into her partner's eyes. "Well, I for one am glad that you did."

If asked, Cheyenne wouldn't have been able to say which of them actually made the first move toward the other, or how she went from sitting there, talking to her partner, to tilting her head toward him and giving in to the wave of overwhelming curiosity that came over her.

Without a hint of a prelude, she found herself kissing her partner.

And enjoying the hell out of it.

At bottom, she knew it wasn't something she should have done, not here, not now. But she definitely was not sorry about it.

Chapter 18

When Jefferson drew his head back and looked at the woman before him, he wasn't sure if he had just wistfully imagined the whole thing, or if it had really happened.

The way his blood was pounding in his veins told him that he hadn't imagined it. He desperately found himself wanting to take what he was feeling to its logical conclusion. But he didn't want to insult his partner and make her think that he was some sort of predator, because he wasn't. Jeff was a man who believed in maintaining a good working relationship and held women in high regard. That being said, he was also extremely attracted to the woman he was working with.

Things had been a great deal simpler in his dad's

day, Jeff thought. His dad had told him, more than
once, about how he had courted his mom. There had
been flowers and quiet, romantic dinners at a little
out-of-the-way restaurant located on the outskirts
of El Paso.

He wasn't sure how Cheyenne would react to any
of that, Jefferson mused. She might think that he was
trying to talk her into something.

The only way to find out was to go ahead and do
it. At least she hadn't read him the riot act for what
had already just transpired between them. That fact
at least gave him a little bit of hope.

"Would you like to come upstairs for a drink?"
he asked, watching her face carefully for a reaction
to his question.

"Yes," Cheyenne answered honestly. "But if I did,
I'd have to hang around for a while. It wouldn't exactly be very responsible of me to drive home with
a high level of alcoholic content in my blood."

He certainly didn't see anything wrong with that.
"You could stay for as long as you felt was necessary
for you to stabilize. Or," he said, offering his partner an
alternative solution, "I could just make you some tea."

Tea, right, she thought. She couldn't see him having any tea on hand for any reason. "You're just fish-
ing for a way to get me upstairs," Cheyenne told him
with an amused smile.

Jeff shrugged noncommittedly in response to her
comment. "I could always bring the tea downstairs
to you," her partner told her. "No harm in that."

"No, upstairs to your apartment will be just fine," she told him. "Besides, it's getting rather chilly out here. Your apartment will be a lot warmer."

She was right. The wind was seeping into the car, Jeff realized, bringing a chill with it. Getting out, he closed the door behind him.

"Upstairs it is," he agreed, rounding the hood of her vehicle. Her partner offered her his arm. After a beat, she took it. "By the way, this is not a comment on my thinking you're being a little unstable. It's just my way of trying to display a little gallantry on my part."

She laughed softly under her breath. "I wasn't taking it as an insult."

They entered the building and the difference between outside and inside was rather amazing, she thought. She stopped shivering the moment she crossed the ground floor and approached the elevator.

"How do you like living here?" she asked her partner, indicating the immediate area.

He assumed she was referring to the living quarters. "It's a lot neater than the place where I used to live when I came home from serving in the Marines. That place was practically just a small cabin and in fact the place was close to being over eighty years old." He shook his head as he remembered the space. "As a matter of fact, it looked every inch of that."

Reaching the second floor, Jefferson got out of the elevator and led the way to his apartment. Unlocking the door, he stepped back to allow her to enter first.

"Go ahead," he told her, bracing himself.

"Go ahead what?" Cheyenne asked, assuming that he wasn't just telling her to walk in, that there was something more involved in viewing the apartment.

"Tell me what's wrong with it," he said.

She looked at him in surprise. "There's nothing wrong with it," she told him. "Oh, it could probably stand a little dusting here and there, but other than that, it looks fine. Tell you this much, you're a lot better at housekeeping than any of my brothers were before they got married."

Her partner smiled at her as he closed the door behind them and flipped the lock. "That's gratifying to hear," Jeff told her.

"Glad I could gratify you," she teased, then she looked slowly around the kitchen. "Where do you keep your coffee?"

He appeared rather surprised at her question. "You're passing on the tea?"

It was her turn to be surprised. "You were serious about the tea?"

"Yes, I was serious," her partner told her. "I offered it to you, didn't I?"

"Well, yes, you did, but to be very honest and even a little sexist, I never knew any man who actually chose to *drink* tea. Coffee or even a trendy latte or two, yes. But tea?" Cheyenne shook her head. "Never."

Jefferson decided that perhaps an explanation might be in order. "When I was a kid, I had a really bad case of the stomach flu. I couldn't keep anything down and I mean *anything*. I just kept throwing up absolutely everything I put in my mouth and tried to swallow. My mother was desperate to help me and as a last resort, she brewed a pot of tea for me to drink.

"I wound up practically living on the stuff," he told his partner. "Eventually, it managed to settle my stomach enough that I was able to keep some food down. Very slowly, I became human again and I gained new respect for the brew."

"What did you wind up having, illness-wise?" she asked her partner, curious.

He could only shrug. "Who knows? We couldn't afford a doctor back then. My mother fell back on using old remedies that she was raised with. Luckily for me, they worked. Because they did, I've had a fondness for tea ever since."

Cheyenne could readily understand that. "Then I'll let you do the honors," she told him, raising her hands in surrender as she backed away from the stove to give him complete access to it.

"All right, then, let me get to it," he told Cheyenne, moving past her to get to the stove. Taking the kettle, he poured water into it, deposited the proper amount of tea leaves into it and started to prepare the beverage for steaming.

"Is there anything you want me to do?" she asked he partner. It wasn't in Cheyenne to just stand around doing nothing. She was used to being perpetually busy. Besides, if she kept busy, she wouldn't feel tempted by her partner, which at the moment, she was. There was just something about the man that seemed to tempt her—especially now.

Jefferson spared her a glance. "Why don't you just make yourself comfortable?"

She knew he'd say that. "Besides that," she responded.

Jefferson's smile widened as his eyes washed over her. "Nothing that can bear repeating in mixed company." And then he caught himself. "I shouldn't have even said that."

In this day and age, every remark made could be held suspect.

Cheyenne appreciated her partner's thoughtfulness. "Don't worry, I won't hold it against you."

The remark tempted him. Jeff found he just couldn't resist asking her, "So what will you hold against me?"

Heaven help her but her heart began to pound really hard in her chest, anticipation managing to send it into double time. Her breathing grew a good deal harder to regulate.

"What do you want me to hold against you?" she asked him, her voice no louder than a whisper. She caught herself shivering as she felt his breath go up and down her spine.

His eyes were already making love to her.

"Guess," he said to her as he turned away from the stove, the water that was about to boil temporarily forgotten about.

With that, he took her into his arms and, ever so slowly, he brought his lips down to hers. The growing hunger within him seemed to just explode in his veins, all but consuming every last bit of him.

Jefferson kissed her over and over again, each time with even more passion than the last. Rather than satiate him, it just made the hunger within him grow to larger and larger proportions.

Her partner found that his head was spinning wildly, making him almost unbelievably dizzy. He didn't remember moving, didn't remember picking her up in his arms and beginning to walk with her toward his bedroom until the teakettle on the stovetop suddenly began whistling to the point that it all but made his teeth rattle. That definitely caught his attention.

When that happened, he stopped kissing her and drew his head away. Her partner smiled into her eyes.

"What?" she asked.

"I think that's nature's way of calling a time-out," Jeff told her.

"Or just telling us to take a breath," she said, amused, "so we don't wind up suffocating."

A thrill danced up and down her spine, making her shiver in anticipation. "Well, if you ask me, I can't think of a better way to go," he told her.

She all but laughed as she shook her head, causing him to ask her in confusion, "What?"

"I just would have never pegged you as being a romantic," she said.

"Funny, neither would I," he admitted, then added, "until just now. Look, I don't want you thinking that I'm pushing things, or rushing them."

Before he could say anything further, Cheyenne placed her finger against his lips, silencing them. When he raised his eyebrows in quizzical surprise, she told him, "I'm not thinking anything at all—except that maybe you talk a little too much."

Jeff took a deep breath. He needed to get this out before he wasn't able to talk. In his opinion, Cheyenne needed to know this. "The way things are in this day and age, I just want you to know—"

Her eyes met his. She could almost read his mind. "I know," she told him quietly in all sincerity. "Trust me, I know."

With that, her partner pulled her into his arms and kissed her, putting his entire heart and soul into that kiss. The next moment, hoping that she understood what he was trying to get across to her, Jefferson picked her up into his arms and carried Cheyenne into his bedroom.

Her heart was pounding hard as Jefferson deposited her onto his bed, placing her as carefully as if he was laying down an angel.

During all this time, his lips hardly left hers.

They were sealed against her in such a way that he wound up lying down against her, absorbing all of her into his very system.

The time for words, Jefferson thought, had passed.

Jefferson ran his hands along every part of her body, memorizing every dip, every warm curve he touched. Taking it all in until it felt as if it became an absolute part of him as well.

When Cheyenne began to unbutton his shirt, pulling the shirttails out of the waistband of his pants, the hunger he was attempting to contain just got completely out of hand. It exploded in his veins, consuming him, feeding the fire that was blazing within him.

Jefferson returned the compliment and she struggled hard not to cry out as mounting desire seemed to shoot throughout her entire body. Especially when he started to undress her, replacing the material that left her body with long, languid, hot kisses that strategically covered her from top to bottom.

He was nibbling on and branding areas that were all but throbbing with each pass of his hot lips along her aching, wanting skin.

Cheyenne twisted and turned beneath him, glorying in the heat his mouth generated along her.

She wanted to retaliate, to repay him, but she could barely move, barely draw in even so much as a lungful of air to help keep her mind from spinning off into oblivion.

"Stop," she begged. "Stop."

He pulled back, concerned. "Am I hurting you?" he asked, afraid he had somehow managed to go too far.

"No," she told him hoarsely.

He didn't understand. "When why—"

"Because I didn't want this to be just one-sided," she answered. And with that, Cheyenne proceeded to lay siege to Jefferson's body, teasing him and branding him to create just a little of the impression that he had managed to leave along her body.

They went on like that for a couple of go-rounds, making each other crazy until they were all but weak with desire, until their bodies were completely throbbing and aching.

And then, finally, unable to resist the final step, Cheyenne turned into her partner, opening herself up to him as her mouth was sealed against his.

She felt Jefferson part her legs beneath him and she caught her breath as he slipped into her.

With her heart pounding, they became engaged in the timeless dance that had seized couples since the very beginning of time.

Their hips began to move faster and faster in time to a song that their bodies had been dancing to since this had begun between them.

Desire exploded within them, absorbing them and eventually leaving them smiling, satisfied and incredibly grateful that this had happened between them.

Without realizing it, they fell asleep in each other's arms, happy and deeply contented. The sound of their breathing mingled until it grew fainter and fainter. Finally the sound faded away as it wound up generating a heart-softening warmth around them.

Chapter 19

The ringing noise penetrated the fog that had descended around Cheyenne's and Jeff's brains. The fog had locked them into a state of sleep that eventually broke apart, thanks to the noise.

They opened their eyes almost simultaneously and looked at one another, trying to orient themselves as well as identifying the source of the ringing.

Rubbing the sleep from her eyes, Cheyenne looked at the man beside her. He was awake, she realized.

Stifling a yawn, she asked her partner, "Is that yours or mine?" Her voice was still somewhat thick with sleep.

"Both, I think," he answered, stifling a yawn of his own.

The ringing noise helped to guide them to where

their phones were lying. Jeff's was on the nightstand next to the lamp while Cheyenne's cell phone was on the floor, just beneath the bed.

Jefferson leaned over her to reach his phone while Cheyenne reached down beneath the bed in order to retrieve hers.

They answered their phones within moments of one another.

Cheyenne was first. When he spoke, she instantly recognized her uncle's voice. Brian Cavanaugh, the chief of d's, was on the other end of the line.

Sitting back up on the bed, she leaned her head against the headboard and pulled her legs in under her. Because of the hour—5:00 a.m.—she abandoned all pretext of formality. Also because of the hour, her mind went instantly to a bad place. Cheyenne's fingertips were cold and she stiffened as she held the phone against her ear.

"Uncle Brian, what's wrong?" she asked nervously.

But when her uncle answered her, it wasn't what she had expected him to say.

"That damn serial killer struck again, Cheyenne," he told her. The chief of d's wasted no time filling her in on the details. "Some hiker making his way through the woods late last night stumbled across a fresh grave. This time the victim's face was just bashed in, not really erased, like the others had been. But there's no doubt in anyone's mind that it's the work of the same man."

Although it made her feel guilty, Cheyenne couldn't

deny that she was relieved to hear that the reason for the call had nothing to do with an emergency involving her uncle or any of the other older members of her family. Dealing with the uglier side of life had her worrying about things closer to home more than she usually did.

"Where?" she asked a bit breathlessly.

From the look on Jefferson's face when she glanced in his direction, he was apparently on the receiving end of a similar call. The Aurora precinct was on the alert.

So much for being able to go back to sleep, Cheyenne thought, resigning herself to the fact that this was the beginning of her day.

As Cheyenne listened, her uncle Brian rattled off the specifics of the crime. She was wide awake now.

"I just sent the medical examiner to the scene where the body was discovered. He's going to collect it and bring the murdered woman back to Autopsy. But he won't do anything until you and your team get there since this has become your case," Brian told her.

She nodded even though she knew that he couldn't see her. "I'll get the others together and we'll be there as soon as we possibly can," Cheyenne promised her uncle.

"I know you will." She heard him let out a long sigh. "Hell of a way to end the evening, isn't it?" the chief of detectives asked her.

"You certainly said a mouthful, Chief," she told

the man as she ended the call. The next moment, she was throwing off the blanket she'd had wrapped around her torso and turning toward the man sitting up beside her. "Looks like duty calls," she said.

"Maybe after we take care of what needs to be done and collect all the necessary information, we might be able to pick up where we left off?" Jeff suggested, raising his brow, a touch of hope in his eyes.

That took her by surprise. Despite the nature of the situation, she could feel a smile forming within her. "Is that what you want to do?" she asked him in complete innocence. After all, there had been no words exchanged between them, no hint of any sort of commitment beyond the moment and the evening.

Jefferson had never been someone who believed in playing any sort of games. Honesty had always been his hallmark and he had always believed in shooting straight from the hip.

It was no different now and he answered her in all honesty.

"Hell, yes." And then he decided to temper his response. After all, he didn't want to scare her away. "Unless you think I'm being too pushy and you just want to take a raincheck on anything else that might be in the offing when we get back from whatever it is that the rest of today might hold for us."

Cheyenne paused for a moment, as if attempting to unscramble what her partner had just said to her. It wasn't in her to jump to conclusions, no matter how much she might be tempted to do just that.

"We'll talk when we get back," she told him. "And for the record," Cheyenne decided to add for good measure, "neither one of us is being too pushy. And I think that if this serial killer had just taught us anything, it's that life should be grabbed and held on to with both hands whenever possible."

With that, Cheyenne rose from his bed, wrapping the blanket around herself. "Now, would you mind if I showered first?" she asked him, making her way toward the bathroom. "I want to get ready and I guarantee that I am really fast."

Jeff grinned at her. The woman really amused him. One way or the other, he intended to let his partner go first. "What kind of a gentleman would I be if I said no?" he asked her with an innocent shrug.

"A cleaner one," Cheyenne commented with a laugh. "Okay, I'll be right out," she promised. She grabbed the rest of her clothes and a towel and made her way into the bathroom to grab a quick shower.

True to her promise, Cheyenne was in and out of the shower—and the bathroom—in what seemed to Jefferson to be lightning speed.

She saw that her partner had just finished brewing their coffee and had just put in four slices of bread into the toaster.

"Your turn," Cheyenne declared as she finished toweling her hair dry.

She had managed to catch Jefferson totally by surprise. "You sure the water even hit you?" he marveled.

Cheyenne laughed. "Yes, I'm very sure. Go take your shower," she urged. Gesturing around the kitchen, she told him, "I'll finish making breakfast."

"Will do," he told her, putting down his knife. "And you don't have to bother making my breakfast," he told her on his way out. "We can pick up something at the diner on the way to the crime scene."

She waved her partner on his way. "Just go take your shower."

Something in her voice caught his attention. "You're not planning on timing me, are you?" he asked, even though he knew there was no way he could possibly compete with her. Her speed had managed to take his breath away.

A smile played on Cheyenne's lips. "Only if you take too long," she answered.

Jefferson paused for a second in the doorway leading into the bathroom. He turned around to look at her. "Then what?" he asked. "You'll come in to drag me out?"

Humor gleamed in her eyes. "I might," she said, her expression remaining unchanged.

Her partner grinned at her, apparently rolling the matter over in his mind. "It might be worth it," he responded with relish.

Cheyenne waved her partner on his way. "Go, shower, get ready. I still have to stop at my place to change my clothes. It might look really suspicious if I turn up at the crime scene wearing the same outfit that I wore to the party yesterday."

"Not suspicious," her partner contradicted. "They'll just think that I was one really lucky son of a gun."

"Go!" Cheyenne ordered, pointing to the bathroom door just behind him.

"Gone," her partner told her, holding his hands up to indicate his surrender as he went into the bathroom to take his shower.

Jefferson walked out of the bathroom some twenty minutes later to the warm, tempting scent of brewed coffee, toast and eggs.

"That smells really good," Jefferson enthused as he closed the door behind him and walked into the kitchen.

"Thank you." She deposited the plate of eggs, bacon and toast in front of him. "Eat fast. I told my uncle we'd be there as soon as possible and I still have to grab a change of clothes at my place."

"We?" he questioned.

"My team," she clarified. "We're all being summoned to the scene and I called them while you were in the shower. They weren't overly happy about the wake-up call."

"I know how they feel," he told her, sitting down at the table. "Aren't you having any?" he asked, noticing that there was no plate in front of her.

"I already ate," she told him.

Jefferson looked at her in total disbelief. "You cooked, notified the rest of the team and ate breakfast all in an incredibly short amount of time." He glanced over his shoulder toward the sink. "And I notice that you washed and dried the frying pan and put it away as well. Wow. I had no idea that you had these superpowers."

"Not superpowers," she corrected. "I can move really fast. I always have been able to. It comes in handy when you're one of nine siblings. Otherwise, you run the risk of going hungry and getting left behind while the others wind up cleaning everything out."

"I never thought of it that way," he admitted with a shrug of his shoulders. "That kind of thing doesn't come up when you're an only child."

"Everything has its advantages and disadvantages," she told her partner. "I guess it all depends on how you look at things." Finished drinking her coffee, Cheyenne rose to her feet, pushing her chair back. "Ready to go?" she asked him as she rinsed out her cup.

He laughed. "I guess I can digest my breakfast on the way there."

Cheyenne smiled at him. "You read my mind."

"Not hardly, but I can definitely make a calculated guess." Her partner looked over toward the counter. "I'm assuming you found my coffee thermos."

Beaming, she placed the full thermos on the table as she whisked away Jefferson's breakfast dish and deposited it into the sink.

"There you go," she told him, nodded at the thermos as she quickly cleaned and rinsed his plate and coffee cup. She had always hated having dishes pile up in the sink.

Jefferson could only shake his head. "I am really impressed."

"Save that," Cheyenne told her partner, "for when we finally find the serial killer and have irrefutable proof that he's our man."

Something about her wording caught his attention. "You're that sure that the killer is a male?" Jefferson asked her.

"Let's just say I'm ninety-nine percent sure," she told him. "Statistics show that most serial killers are males and white, which is why both males of color and females usually slip under the radar and elude capture for a long time if they have the misfortune of actually being guilty. And sometimes," she added unhappily, "they even manage to get away with the crime."

There was admiration in his eyes as he looked at his partner. "Working with you is proving to be a real education," Jefferson told her, then confessed, "I never counted on that when I came here."

Cheyenne beamed at her partner. "I do my best," she replied. "All right, follow me in your car. That way we can tell my uncle and the others that I swung around to bring you to the scene of the murder since you still don't know your way around the area. It'll explain why we arrived more or less at the same time. Don't worry, I'll change my clothes really fast."

At this point, he had no reason to doubt her. "You

really do seem to have everything covered," Jeff marveled.

She smiled at him as she got into her vehicle. "This is not my first rodeo," she told her partner.

"I wouldn't have thought that it was," he told her, then asked, "How long did you say you've been on the police force?"

"I've been on the force for five years," she told him. "However, I've been a Cavanaugh all my life. You learn things by observing. Being a Cavanaugh family member is an education all on its own." Taking out her key, Cheyenne pointed it toward the car. All four locks sprang open. "Ready?"

Her partner quickly followed suit, opening his own car door. "Ready," he declared.

"Then let's go," she told him.

With that, Cheyenne got in behind the wheel of her vehicle. In less than a moment, she was ready to lead the way to her place.

Chapter 20

The edge of the forest where the latest victim had been found was swimming with police personnel moving in all directions. Along with officers, a medical examiner and his assistant as well as several other people who worked for the police department, a number of detectives who had been attached to the serial killer cold case, appeared on the scene.

After they reached the area, Cheyenne and her partner had parked their cars and made their way to the center of the group.

Cheyenne went to the first person she knew was working the case. "What do we have, Dr. Barlow?" Cheyenne asked the medical examiner.

"Offhand I'd say that it looks like our guy didn't

get a chance to savor his handiwork," the medical examiner said answering her question.

The man was standing over the body that had just been placed on the gurney, looking rather pensive.

"What makes you say that?" Jefferson asked. He glanced in his partner's direction, a silent apology on his face for usurping her by asking the question first. But he was really curious.

"All the other dead women who we found had their clothing carefully removed as well as their facial features all but erased and bashed in. I think in this case, the serial killer was surprised in the middle of what he was doing and was forced to do a hasty cover-up. Her grave was an extremely shallow one. It turned out to be hardly deep enough to even cover her," the doctor said. There was pity in his voice as he shook his head, gazing down at the victim.

"Do we have any idea who the victim was yet?" Cheyenne asked. How could anyone do such an awful thing once, much less several times? She just couldn't bring herself to understand it.

"Not yet, but like I said, I think our killer got sloppy this time around because he was in a hurry. Her fingerprints weren't all rubbed away and as for her facial features, he didn't eliminate them in his customary manner by bashing her face in. My guess is that the serial killer feels cheated and deprived and unless I really miss my guess, he's undoubtedly going to strike again in order to try to satisfy his hunger," the medical examiner pointed out.

If the killer had gotten sloppy, maybe that meant there were clues that were left behind. "Did the killer leave behind any telltale evidence we might be able to use?" Cheyenne asked.

"Nothing that I can see, but your team and the people assisting them haven't finished going through all the evidence that was left behind. Granted this was still a terrible crime, but maybe we'll get lucky this time," the medical examiner said hopefully.

Cheyenne frowned. "'Getting lucky' in my book would mean that there would be no killers, serial or otherwise," Cheyenne told the older man.

The medical examiner paused as he started to pack up his medical bag, preparing to go back to Autopsy with the body. He looked at Cheyenne intently. A hint of a smile played on his lips.

"They told me that you were an optimist. I guess they were right beyond their wildest dreams," Dr. Barlow speculated.

"Looking for the good in people is hardly being optimistic. It's just being hopeful." Cheyenne could feel her partner as well as the medical examiner looking at her. She, meanwhile, was looking down at the draped body lying on the gurney. "Poor woman, the killer not only stripped her of her clothes, but of her dignity as well." Anger creased her features. "If I could get my hands on the scum, it would be really hard not to give in to the temptation to choke the life out of this heartless creep," she told the medical examiner as well as her partner.

Jefferson laughed warily. "Remind me never to get on the wrong side of you," he told his partner.

Cheyenne gave him a spasmodic smile that he had absolutely no idea how to read. "Don't do anything wrong and there won't be a problem," she told her partner.

A warm feeling came over him as he thought of last night and making love with her. Despite the nature of the crime they were dealing with, thoughts of last night had left him in an excellent place mentally. "That's easier said than done," he told her.

They remained in the immediate area, working the crime scene and dealing with the evidence for a good long while, until everything had been packed up and as accounted for as humanly possible.

By day's end it was easy to see that everyone felt weary from the inside out. "That makes at least four victims that we know of," Cheyenne told her partner. "And who knows how many others have been killed that we haven't been able to find—or how many this killer has eliminated and disposed of that we haven't found yet." She shivered as she turned the matter over in her mind. "For all we know, this serial killer hasn't contained his killing spree to just one area. Who knows how far his reach has extended?"

"You know what I said about you being an optimist?" her partner asked her.

She watched as her team packed up and withdrew from the scene, more than ready to call it a day. "Yes?"

A hint of a smile teased his lips. "I think I've changed my mind about that," Jefferson told her.

Cheyenne laughed softly. "I guess that you're entitled," she told him.

"Are you hungry?" her partner asked Cheyenne. "I don't think we've eaten since you made breakfast early this morning," he pointed out.

She thought for a moment. "You know, I think you're right. I just got so caught up in this awful crime, I guess I wound up losing my appetite."

"Well, the way I see it," her partner said, "you need to keep up your strength or we won't be able to bring this creep down. Say, why don't I buy you dinner tonight? You name the place."

She wasn't trying to be coy, Cheyenne thought. Her appetite really did feel as if it was missing in action.

At this point, they were walking to their vehicles. Instead of answering her partner, Cheyenne thought for a moment, mentally taking inventory of the contents of her refrigerator. And then she looked at him as a solution hit her.

"I've got a couple of steaks in my refrigerator. Why don't I make them and we can have that? After spending all day around a bunch of people on this new case, I really don't feel up to going out to a restaurant and listening to people talk and exchange pleasantries with one another around us."

"Aren't you the one who said we shouldn't allow this to get to us?" her partner reminded her.

Cheyenne pressed her lips together, doing her best to try to raise her spirits. "You're right," she told Jefferson. "If I let this get to me, I'm not going to be of any good to anyone." And that, she silently added, wouldn't be very responsible of her, nor would it help the victims or their families. She was a Cavanaugh and had a reputation to maintain.

Because there was no one around them and they were basically alone inside her vehicle, Cheyenne leaned over to brush her lips against his cheek. The move on her part managed to take him completely by surprise.

Jefferson ran his fingertips against his cheek, tracing the outline of her kiss and almost pressing it into his skin. "Well, I wouldn't exactly say that you wouldn't be any good to anyone," he responded, then dropped his hand from his face. "Does this mean that we're going steady?"

She laughed out loud at his reference. "I don't think I've heard that line being used in a very long time."

He blew out a breath as Cheyenne stepped on the gas and they took off, driving to her house.

"Maybe if we attempted to go back to the way things once were in the past, things might actually get better," Jefferson told her.

She spared him a look. "I totally agree, but right now, we need to focus on the immediate case and get this sick individual off our streets," she said with feeling. This killer was making her sick to her stomach.

"Amen to that," her partner responded. He decided to give it one last try. "Are you sure you don't want me to buy dinner for us?"

"I'm sure. Besides, cooking always manages to relax me," she added by way of an explanation.

The remark had her partner laughing in response.

She looked at him, confused and somewhat mystified as to what struck him as being so funny. "What's so funny?" Cheyenne asked.

"I was just thinking about my late mother's reaction to cooking. She used to complain whenever she had to even boil water." Jefferson smiled to himself. "My mother was a really warm, loving person but cooking definitely was not her forte."

"Well, cooking as a passion runs in my family," Cheyenne reminded her partner. "You met my uncle Andrew. He acted like he was being punished when he had to keep out of the kitchen," she pointed out to Jefferson.

Her partner nodded in response. "You Cavanaughs definitely are a very unique breed of people."

She smiled as she drove the rest of the way to her house. "I won't argue with that."

Reaching her destination, Cheyenne pulled up and left her vehicle parked in front of her house.

Getting out, Jefferson looked at her. "You don't park your car in the garage?" he asked, curious. If he had a garage, he would have parked his vehicle in it all the time.

"This makes jumping into my car and taking off a lot easier," she told him.

He frowned, trying to make sense out of what she was telling him. "Is that a regular thing? Jumping into your car and having to take off?"

"Once or twice," she allowed, then added, "I just like being prepared for all contingencies."

"I don't think I've ever met anyone quite like you," her partner told Cheyenne.

"Is that a good thing or a bad thing?" she asked.

His eyes smiled at her as he put his arm around her shoulders to usher her into her house. "At the risk of possibly scaring you off, I'd say that it's definitely a very good thing."

She nodded in response. "Make yourself comfortable. The steaks should be ready in fifteen minutes—or less," Cheyenne hedged.

"Sounds good," he told her. "Anything you'd like me to do?"

"Just sit there and look pretty," she told him with an inviting smile. His stomach growled rather loudly just then. Her smile grew into a grin. "And try to be patient," she added, glancing down at his stomach.

"I'll do my best," Jefferson promised. "Do you have anything to drink?"

Cheyenne got busy preparing the steaks. She enumerated what she knew was currently in her refrigerator. "I have ginger ale, orange juice, the ever-present water and there's half a bottle of red wine on the back shelf from about six months ago."

"I take it that you took the instruction to 'sip slowly' to heart," he told her with a laugh.

"Let's put it this way. If I'm going to drink something alcoholic, it would be something tastier, like along the lines of a sloe gin fizz or something with an equally cute name," she said. "I don't drink alone and usually when I come home, I'm too tired to do anything but fall asleep," she told him as she continued to go through the steps of preparing the steak. "How do you like your steak?"

"Barely dead," he told her honestly.

Her brow furrowed. "Do you want me to take that literally?" Cheyenne asked him.

"Absolutely," he answered. "I've always had a weakness for rare meat."

"Barely dead it is," she told him, turning up the flame beneath the frying pan.

"Shouldn't it be lower?" he asked her, nodding at the stove top.

"It'll be done faster this way," she told him.

He looked at the flame beneath the frying pan. "As long as you don't burn down the house along the way."

"Hasn't happened yet," she told him with satisfaction. "Relax and let me do my thing."

Jeff inclined his head and saluted her. "You got it."

Her eyes crinkled as she beamed at him. "Good answer."

Chapter 21

After spending the night together—something that was becoming a habit although Cheyenne didn't intend to raise that point if Jefferson did not—she and her partner went to the precinct to do some further research on the case, the same thing that they did the following day. And the day after that.

Cheyenne was determined to use every single resource available to them, hoping that somehow, by using what was available, they could find and identify the serial killer in order to stop the man in his tracks. They needed to find a way to keep the man from killing more defenseless older women. She was positive that the killer was attempting to fill some sort of imaginary quota he had come up with for himself. Where had it come from?

"Not that it actually matters whether these women are older or younger," Cheyenne muttered. "This animal has absolutely no business killing anyone. What kind of scum thinks he has the right to deprive someone of their life, no matter how he tries to justify what he's doing?"

Jeff looked up at the woman from where he was sitting at his desk. He thought that the question she was asking was a rhetorical one.

"If we could answer that, we could very well wind up unscrambling the mystery of the universe," her partner told her. "Or at least come damn close to actually solving that mystery."

Cheyenne leaned back in her chair as she momentarily closed her eyes. "I cannot tell you how frustrating all this is, going around in circles and, for the moment, feeling as if I'm getting absolutely nowhere."

Jeff laughed shortly. "You don't have to tell me," her partner said. "I'm right there right next to you, remember?"

Opening her eyes again, Cheyenne nodded as her eyes met his. She hadn't meant to sound disparaging or depressed, although having this killer out there was getting to her. She needed to shut her mind to that part of this ordeal.

"Sorry. Sometimes it just helps to say things out loud," she told her partner, trying to explain her way of thinking.

The next moment, her eyes were drawn toward the department doorway. There was a police officer escorting a woman into their department. It was the same woman who had come to them the other day, asking them to find the whereabouts of her missing mother. Cheyenne exchanged glances with her partner, bracing herself for the same questions. Namely, did they have any word about the woman's missing mother? So far, they didn't.

In Cheyenne's opinion there were two terrible things about this job that she was so dedicated to working. The first, of course, was having to inform a person that their loved one was never going to be coming home again. That was akin to taking a knife and carving up their insides. The second was telling a person that they had no new news to tell them about any sort of development in a missing persons case. The hopeless look in their eyes always got to her, Cheyenne thought.

The case she and Jeff were working was still in the latter realm.

To her relief, Jeff greeted the woman before she came over to her desk to ask her that awful question.

"No, I'm sorry, Ms. Richardson, there's been no new news about your mother's whereabouts as of yet, but we still haven't given up," Jefferson told her.

The woman looked at the two detectives, appearing rather nervous about what she was about to impart. "I might be able to help with that," she finally told them.

Cheyenne exchanged looks with her partner. She

knew better than to allow herself to get carried away or become unrealistically hopeful.

"Please, have a seat, Ms. Richardson," Cheyenne urged, gesturing the woman over toward a nearby free chair. When the woman sat down, Cheyenne asked, "What is it that you have for us?"

The missing woman's daughter appeared to be even more nervous. "I'm almost embarrassed to tell you this."

"Please, Ms. Richardson, we are way past the point of embarrassment here," Jefferson assured the woman. "The only important thing here is for us to be able to find your mother."

Cheyenne noted that, mercifully, he did not say anything about finding out what *happened* to her mother, but simply said that they needed to find the woman—which she thought sounded a great deal more encouraging and comforting.

Meanwhile, the woman in question's daughter nodded in response. "The reason I'm here was that I was trying to comfort myself by going through my mother's things. I was looking through them in order to reacquaint myself with the kind of person my mother was." She sighed. "As it turns out, there are things about my mother I never knew."

Cheyenne's interest was instantly piqued. "Such as?" she asked, waiting to be enlightened.

"Such as I never knew that my mother enlisted in the Army straight out of high school. Something must have happened that she wasn't happy about or proud of because she never said anything about that to either my sister or to me. Not only that, but she did it under another name. The only way I knew it was her was because she used an old photograph that I recognized."

She frowned sadly. "I always thought my mother was the most honest person on the face of the earth. From what I can tell, it looks like I was wrong about that," she told the detectives, embarrassed.

"You don't know that for a fact yet," Jeff told the woman. "There could be a lot of reasons that explain your mother keeping this information to herself and from you."

"According to what I could piece together from her various entries, she left the service because my father, who she wound up marrying at the time, didn't want her to serve in the army. I only found this out by reading entries in a diary she kept—a diary I didn't even know she had." She stopped to look from one detective to the other. She was quite distraught. "Apparently," she said unhappily, "there were a great many things about my mother that I didn't know. She was a totally different person from the one who I thought I knew."

"Don't feel too badly," Jeff told the woman in a sympathetic voice. "Everybody has their secrets."

"The important thing," Cheyenne was quick to point out, "is that as a former soldier, her DNA is registered in a database. We can use that information to identify your mother no matter what name she was using."

"You're talking about one of the people you have lying in your morgue," the woman guessed unhappily.

"Not necessarily," Jeff stressed.

That response caused the woman to brighten more than a little bit, looking really hopeful for the first time since she had walked into their department.

"Really?" Richardson asked. "You can actually do that?"

"Absolutely." Cheyenne's eyes met the woman's. "We can bring this information—the DNA—to the woman who runs our computer lab," she said, thinking of her cousin Valri, who everyone in the precinct regarded as being a complete computer wizard. "Her hobby is working miracles on the side."

The woman's face practically lit up. "If this woman has an answer, you'll call me?" the woman all but begged. "Night or day, I don't care what time it is, or if the news turns out to be good or bad, promise that you'll call me." Her eyes went from one detective to the other, begging them to say yes.

Despite all his lectures to the contrary, he was allowing this case to get to him, Jefferson thought. But he really couldn't pretend otherwise. He knew what the woman was experiencing and what she had to be going through during this trying time. "We will call you," Jeff promised.

The corners of the woman's mouth curved as a

second wave of relief washed over her, all but stealing her breath. "I'll be waiting for your call."

"As soon as we know something—anything at all," Cheyenne underscored, "we will call." She knew the kind of hell that the uncertainty had to be generating within her.

With that, Jeff escorted the woman to the door, turning her over to the police officer who had brought her up to the department today in the first place.

Cheyenne was smiling at her partner when he turned around to face her. "What?" he asked uncertainly, immediately noticing her expression.

"Nothing. It's just that you turned out to be a real softie," she told him. "I wasn't prepared for that," she admitted.

Jefferson didn't look happy about the description. "I resent that," he told her.

"Resent it all you want. It doesn't change a thing. It's still true," she told him with a smile totally softening her features. She saw a protest forming on her partner's lips and quickly said, "You're turning out to be a much better guy than I thought you would."

"You didn't think I'd be a good partner?" he asked her, somewhat surprised by her admission.

"Well, you did seem a little cocky when you first came in," she reminded him even though it wasn't all that long ago.

"Cocky?" Jeff echoed, putting a hand to his chest and feigning overwhelming surprise. "Me?"

"I know, I know, what was I thinking?" she responded with an amused laugh. "All right," she said, moving on, "let's see if we can find that woman's DNA and then turn that over to Valri to see if she can find a match to a female soldier. That match just might pair up with one of the bodies that're lying in Autopsy. Or," she went on, thinking best-case scenario, "we find out that her DNA *doesn't* match one of the bodies in Autopsy and that woman's mother is actually alive somewhere."

Listening, Jeff shook his head as the magnitude of the investigation hit him. "This case is getting really complex," he said with a deep sigh.

"No, on the contrary, at last it's finally pointing to some sort of a resolution. Maybe with this new input, we now stand a decent chance of getting this creature off the streets and behind bars—preferably in solitary confinement," Cheyenne added, frowning as she thought about the serial killer who was haunting their streets. "And maybe, just maybe, reuniting a mother and daughter in a positive way."

Jeff nodded. "All right, let's see if we can finally start the process of putting this guy's heinous killing spree to an end."

"I'm on board for that," Cheyenne said, leading her partner down toward the computer lab.

Valri Cavanaugh Brody was in the process of attempting to resolve several of the problems that had been dropped on her desk during the course of the last twenty-four hours. When she heard someone entering her lab, she reluctantly glanced up, sensing yet another problem coming her way and being dropped in her lap.

"Oh Lord, I know that look," she groaned when she saw who it was. "It's a 'put me at the head of the line because I'm a Cavanaugh' look," Valri lamented.

"Actually, it's an 'I've got a simple problem' look," Cheyenne explained to her cousin.

Valri looked past Cheyenne toward the man who had come in with her.

"Hi, I'm Valri," she said, introducing herself to the man she hadn't met as of yet. "And you are…?"

"Cheyenne's new partner, Jefferson McDougall," Jefferson said, stepping forward to shake Valri's hand. He remembered seeing her at Andrew Cavanaugh's birthday party, but only at a distance.

Valri smiled at the man. "Well, you seem to be holding up well. What can I do for you?" she asked, directing her question toward the new partner as a courtesy.

"We need you to access some old military records so that you can tell us what this former soldier's name is," Cheyenne said, cutting in. "We have her DNA, thanks to her daughter."

"Am I allowed to ask why?" Valri asked, glancing at the name, which struck her as being rather generic.

"We think that it might help us identify the body that's lying in the morgue," Jeff told her.

"Or let us know that it's *not* that person," Cheyenne told her cousin.

"Does it have anything to do with the current serial killer case?" Valri asked.

"It has *everything* to do with the serial killer case," Cheyenne told her cousin.

Valri put her hand out for the information. "By all means, bring it on. Anything to capture this hateful killer."

"My sentiments exactly." Cheyenne handed over the folder with the information she had just printed up. "I figured that you could give us the most amount of information in the fastest amount of time."

Valri opened up the folder. Looking at what was inside, she said, "That would be a very pleasant change." She quickly looked at the name that had been supplied, then keyed it into the appropriate area on her screen to see what she could find.

Ten minutes later, using the information that had been supplied, Valri had managed to locate the person that Cheyenne and her partner had been looking for.

"The former soldier's name is Lauren Master. Her DNA is AB negative." She looked up at her cousin. "AB negative is pretty rare."

"That makes it easier to identify the victim, right?" Jeff asked the woman.

"As long as you can match it to one of the victims tucked away in the autopsy drawer," she told the duo. The printer next to her computer came to life, printing out the information she had just accessed and had now keyed into the screen. Once it was printed, Valri handed the single sheet that had emerged out of her printer to Cheyenne. "There you go," she declared. "And please keep me apprised of how this case goes. I want to see this guy be put away."

Cheyenne looked at her cousin in amazement. "I've never seen you get caught up in a case before," she told her cousin.

"I have to restrain myself," Valri told her in all honesty. "Otherwise, I'd never be able to fall asleep. These kind of things will just prey on my mind and never leave me alone."

"Well, good luck," she added, calling after the detectives as they left her lab.

"That went well," Jeff said to his partner as they went down the hallway to the stairs.

"Hold off on that until the medical examiner tells us we have a match," she cautioned Jefferson.

Jefferson saluted his partner. "Will do," he told Cheyenne.

Chapter 22

"Kristin?" Cheyenne said in surprise as she and her partner Jefferson walked into the room where the autopsies were performed.

Cheyenne looked around the imposing area, looking for the man she thought of as a slightly oversized gremlin. Adrian Barlow, the medical examiner, was nowhere to be seen.

"Where's Dr. Barlow?" Cheyenne asked the young woman at the desk who had been busy writing notes for a file when they had walked in.

"Not here," her cousin-in-law told the detectives. "He had a family emergency. So I'm afraid that you're stuck with me," the attractive young woman wearing hospital fatigues told the two detectives.

"I wouldn't exactly call getting the best medical examiner in the county, maybe the state, 'being stuck,'" Cheyenne said to Dr. Kristin Alberghetti Cavanaugh. "Truth be told, you are definitely my favorite medical examiner by far." She turned toward her partner and said, "She's extremely competent, very easy to talk to and on top of that, she married Malloy, one of my former playboy cousins, domesticating him. That brought a huge sense of relief to my uncle."

Kristin grinned at the narrative. "Occasionally, when the spirit moves me, I walk on water as well," the medical examiner teased. She put a hand out toward Cheyenne's partner. "Hi, you must be Cheyenne's new partner. I believe I saw you at Uncle Andrew's party the other night."

"Probably," Jeff agreed. "There were an awful lot of faces swimming around in front of me. It was hard to keep everyone straight," he said by way of an apology.

Cheyenne flashed a wide smile at the medical examiner. "He flunked the quiz at the end of the evening, but I decided to give him another chance." She became serious. "We're actually here to possibly help you identify one of the serial killer victims who might be lying here."

Rising, Kristin led the way over to the drawers that were against the wall. "Bring it on, I'm all ears," she said, looking at the duo. "What have you got for me and how did you come by the information?"

"It's actually a rather unusual story," Cheyenne admitted. "The young woman who initially came to us about her missing mother said she was going through her mother's things the other evening when she discovered that the woman who had raised her, who she thought she knew like the back of her hand, was once enlisted in the army."

Kristin's eyes immediately lit up at the information. "The military. That means that her DNA has to be filed somewhere in some database," she declared with no small degree of excitement.

Cheyenne grinned back at the woman. "Exactly. Even though there are no fingerprints or identifying facial features, you can't just eliminate DNA out of the victim's system at will."

"And you do have the woman's DNA?" Kristin asked, not about to assume anything.

Cheyenne unfolded the note she had, which contained the woman's military name, her record as well as her DNA on it. "Everything is right here," she said, placing the paper on the table right in front of the medical examiner.

Kristin picked up the paper, looking at it. "AB negative," she read, then murmured, "That's rare." She looked up at the two people in the room with her. "It's going to take me a little while to run the test to determine her DNA," she told them. When the detectives made no move to leave, Kristin found herself telling her cousin-in-law and the woman's partner, "I work better without having my every move scrutinized closely."

"I think that's our cue to leave," Jefferson said,

not overly happy about the fact. "So when would you want us to come back?"

"It takes from two to five days to run the test," Kristin informed the duo. "Sometimes longer." She heard her cousin as well as Jefferson groan at the news. "But I have a friend who knows someone who might be able to speed things up. I will let you know how things go. I just want you to know that I don't need to stand over the lab slide waiting for the results to materialize. I can do other things in the lab while the results are fermenting—so to speak."

"So close and yet so far," Cheyenne murmured with a deep sigh.

Amused, Kristin laughed. "Welcome to my world," she told the two detectives. "Now shoo." She waved Cheyenne and her cousin-in-law's partner on their way. "Let me get started on this."

"Be sure to call me if you need anything, Kristin. Anything at all," Cheyenne emphasized pointedly.

"Oh, don't worry, I will," Kristin told her cousin-in-law in all seriousness.

"I'm beginning to understand the meaning of the phrase 'hurry up and wait,'" Jefferson told his partner as they walked out of Autopsy and headed into the hallway. He clearly looked rather disappointed. "I thought that being as connected as you are, the process to get answers would go a lot faster."

"Maybe faster," she allowed, "but it's still a process. There's only so much that can be done to make the process move along."

"Okay," her partner agreed, resigned. For now it was obvious that there was nothing more that could be done. "So what is our next step?"

She smiled at Jefferson. The man obviously did not like remaining idle any more than she did. She liked that about him. They really were going to get along, she decided, which was a good thing.

Cheyenne thought for a moment and came up with a solution as to how to handle their inertia. "We could return to Aurora Valley to see if we can catch that lecturer we weren't able to corner on Friday. Maybe this time we'll be able to talk to him about that student of his who seems to have gone AWOL, find out if he knows anything about it or has an opinion on the subject."

"Even if we do manage to catch him in, this so-called 'professor' might not want to talk to us," Jefferson pointed out. It was a gut feeling he had, but he didn't want to call it that, given what she had said about some of her family's feelings about the subject.

Cheyenne's eyes narrowed as she thought of the lecturer possibly attempting to avoid her questions if it came down to that. Her eyebrows almost touched, forming an angry vee.

"Oh, he'll talk to us," she told her partner pointedly. "I guarantee he'll talk."

To her surprise, her partner laughed at her tone. "You certainly are a tough little cookie, aren't you?"

Cheyenne thought of all the years that she had competed against her older brothers, going up against them in all sorts of different scenario. She had to admit that it had wound up hardening her and making her that much more determined to win.

"Oh, you don't even know the half of it," she told him with no small amount of conviction.

Something in his partner's voice caught Jeff's attention, causing him to have questions about the woman next to him. "Maybe," he granted, "but I do know that I'd certainly like to find out more."

His words and the expression on his face sent a warm shiver all through her.

Her eyes met his as she smiled. "We can talk about that once we get back tonight."

Back tonight. That definitely sounded promising, her partner thought. Jefferson flashed a smile at her. "Sounds good to me," he told her.

They drove to the college using Cheyenne's vehicle. The campus seemed to be in the middle of shifting from the students who frequented the college in a full-time capacity in the daytime to the students who could only attend classes on a part-time, after-hours basis because they needed to be employed in order to pay for the classes they were taking.

Siting in the passenger seat, Jeff was able to look around the campus and take in the surrounding area. It made more of an impression on him now than it had the first time they had come to check the campus out.

Cheyenne got the impression that there was something on his mind. "What?" she asked him as she guided her car farther into the campus.

"If you ask me, this looks like the perfect area for a crime," Jefferson told her with feeling.

"That's only because you know what might have gone down here," Cheyenne said as she guided her vehicle into an available parking space. "We don't really have any proof to substantiate that," she pointed out.

"Granted that does help add to the aura," Jeff agreed, getting out of Cheyenne's car.

"And seeing how deserted this particular part of the campus is right now just adds to the sense that something less than uplifting could have gone down here," Cheyenne said to him. She turned toward her partner. "Am I right?"

"You, Cheyenne, are always right," he told her.

She looked at him, curiosity etched into her features. "When did I go from 'Cavanaugh' to 'Cheyenne'?"

He smiled broadly at her. "I'd say sometime during our second night together." His eyes were shining at the memory of that night.

"Well, that certainly wasn't coy," she concluded, looking at him.

"I wasn't aware that you were looking for me to be coy," he told Cheyenne.

She drew her shoulders back, bracing herself as they approached the building where they knew their possible suspect was supposed to be teaching in a few hours.

"Right now, what I want," she told her partner, "is to find our possible suspect where he's supposed to be and get him to answer a few questions that we're going to ask him."

"I just want to get him to confess his part in all this if he's actually guilty," her partner said.

"Yes, there's that, too," Cheyenne responded, pushing the door open.

As she did so, Jefferson put his hand up against it and held it for her so she could walk through the entrance and into the ground-floor lobby.

"I guess they don't believe in putting up the heat," he observed, noticing how chilly it felt inside the building. It didn't feel all that different than it did outside.

"Why should they do that?" she asked, pretending to sound surprised. "These are the evening and part-time students who are coming in. They're used to having to put up with hardships," Cheyenne pointed out. "By and large, they are a hardier breed than the ones who attend the school during the day."

Jefferson had trouble containing his laughter. "A little prejudiced are we?"

"I'm not prejudiced," she told him with indignation. "I've just had some experience dealing with privileged kids—the ones who never had to work for anything that they got. I have to admit that I don't exactly think very kindly of them."

"I've had to deal with those types as well," her partner admitted. "But you can't let those types get to you or it'll wind up eating your insides."

She glanced at her partner, clearly impressed with his attitude. "You're more intuitive than I thought you were."

Having him assigned as her new partner had obviously been a good development, Cheyenne thought. She really needed to tell her uncle Brian that she was grateful to him for his forethought and insight.

As they approached Professor Murphy's classroom, they saw movement inside the room via the dark-inted window. There appeared to be only one person visible through the opaque window. The professor? Or was it someone else?

"Looks like we're on," Cheyenne told her partner in a lowered tone of voice.

Jefferson didn't answer. A look came over his face. A cold look that told Cheyenne she wouldn't have wanted to run into the man in the middle of a battlefield when he had been a Marine.

"Looks like," her partner said under his breath.

Cheyenne glanced at her watch. "Class hasn't started yet. This is the perfect time. Let's go," she urged.

They didn't bother knocking on the classroom door—they just walked in.

As if sensing that something was off, the evening lecturer's eyes immediately looked toward the door.

His expression hardened as he seemed to all but shut down right in front of them.

Murphy didn't really look at the man who had crossed the threshold and entered his domain. But the woman was another matter entirely.

He recognized her from a news story he had caught on TV the other day. She was the one that certain sources speculated was trying to find information on a serial killer that people feared was haunting the area and might even be attempting to kill older victims specifically.

The speculation almost made him smile.

Almost.

It looked as if they might be onto him after all this time. Ah well, Murphy always knew that it couldn't last forever, but he had no intention of going quietly, he thought, his face darkening again.

"You're not in my class," he said. He made it sound like an accusation.

"No, we're not," Cheyenne said, taking out her ID and holding it up for his benefit. Jefferson followed suit with his ID. "My partner and I are detectives with the Aurora Police Department and we have a few questions to ask you."

Rage clawed at his throat, all but choking him, although the lecturer's expression didn't change.

The witch who had just sauntered into his classroom had a tone that reminded him of the way his aunt Lily used to sound when she spoke. Like she was in charge of the situation, pretending to be all-knowing.

And that, he thought, struggling to blanket his fury, was going to be this woman's downfall, just the way it had been with his aunt.

A downfall, the lecturer promised himself, he intended to enjoy immensely as he brought it about.

Apparently, Christmas was coming early this year.

Murphy caught himself smiling as he stifled a chuckle.

Chapter 23

Jon Murphy gestured toward the empty seats in the row that was right in front of him. Cheyenne noticed that those seats were lower than the one that the lecturer was sitting in. Most likely to give him a feeling of superiority, she guessed.

"Sit," the lecturer said in a less-than-inviting tone of voice. "What questions would you like me to answer for you?"

Jefferson sensed that the lecturer would respond more to him than he would to Cheyenne. Hoping that his partner wouldn't feel that he was attempting to usurp her, he forged ahead and asked the professor, "We understand that you had a Lauren Dixon in your class until recently."

"I did," the lecturer answered. He waited to see

who or what the two people would bring up next, if anything. Confident in himself, he felt as if he was prepared to tackle anything.

Jefferson wanted to be sure that he had gotten the matter straight. "But she's not in your class anymore?" Cheyenne's partner questioned.

"No, she's not," the lecturer answered the detective, his voice echoing with finality. Mentally, he dared the two detectives to attempt to trip him up.

"Did she decide to take a leave of absence or just drop out of your class or…?" Cheyenne let her voice just drift away, deciding that she had said enough. She was curious to discover just what Murphy would answer.

"Since I have no idea why she is no longer attending my class, I suppose that the best answer to that would be 'or,'" Murphy told the detectives questioning him. For good measure, he decided to add, "It's a shame, really, because she struck me as having the makings of a good student whenever she did speak up in class. And the one paper she handed in was very well written. It did show me that she was able to think on her feet when the occasion called for it."

Cheyenne glanced at her partner. The professor was being rather generous in his praise. That did surprise her. Had they made a mistake suspecting the man? she wondered.

Or was he just trying to hide his true feelings toward the older woman?

"Would you happen to have that paper of hers on file?" Cheyenne asked the lecturer, curious.

Murphy shook his head. "I'm afraid not. I handed back all the papers after I graded and recorded them. I was certain that reviewing her own work would definitely encourage Ms. Dixon," he told the detectives. "Obviously not. Years on the job and I'm still being educated."

Something just didn't ring right to Cheyenne although she couldn't quite put her finger on exactly what was wrong. Maybe, she told herself, she was just being prejudiced against the man. It was as if she was so intent on finding the serial killer who was out there, her mind had been made up even before she ever met the lecturer, although she wasn't usually so dead set against a possible murder suspect. Maybe she had become jaded.

Or maybe she was right.

As if reading his partner's mind, Jeff asked the lecturer point-blank, "Did Ms. Dixon seem to be a little off or preoccupied to you?"

Murphy began to respond and it seemed as if he was about to agree with the assessment the male detective had made, but then apparently he changed his mind about the answer he was about to give.

"I'd like to say yes, but you have to understand that I have a lot of students attending my classes and unless one of them does something noteworthy or outstanding, I'm afraid they just fall through the cracks for me or meld with the other students," Murphy told the two detectives.

The lecturer made a show of glancing at his watch. It was almost time to begin the class. "Looks like your time's up," he told the duo. He almost regretted that. He did enjoy baiting and matching wits with the police, especially when one of them was a woman. The female detective definitely deserved to be put in her place. "Tell you what, why don't you give me your cards," he suggested, "and if I think of anything, anything at all, I'll give one of you a call."

Jefferson was quick to produce his card. Maybe he was being overly protective of his partner, but he didn't want her having to deal with the lecturer. Quite honestly, the man just gave him the creeps. There just seemed to be something off about Jon Murphy and despite the little time he and Cheyenne had had together, he could sense that she saw the man as being a challenge.

To his consternation, he saw Cheyenne produce a card a beat ahead of him. He held it out to the lecturer. Murphy took her card first, although the lecturer did take Jeff's card as well.

The man tucked both cards into his pocket.

"If anything occurs to me, I'll be sure to call," Murphy promised again, a sick, oily smile gracing his lips. The words made Jefferson sick to his stomach.

Jefferson noticed that the lecturer was looking at Cheyenne as he made the promise about calling. It left Jefferson with an admittedly uneasy feeling, not to mention a rather sour taste in his mouth.

"Then it's settled. We'll be waiting to hear from you," Jefferson told the lecturer with finality. And with that, he placed his hand against the small of Cheyenne's back, ushering his partner out of the lecture room and out into the hallway.

"I remember where the hall is, Jefferson. I don't need to be guided like some lost child," Cheyenne told her partner. It was all she could do not to swing around and face him as she made her annoyed accusation.

"Nobody said that you did," Jeff told her. He pressed his lips together, making an effort to choose his words carefully. He didn't want to get into an argument with the woman.

Finally, he decided to just say what was on his mind. "Did you get the same uncomfortable feeling about that guy as I just did?"

Cheyenne chewed on her lower lip, thinking. "I don't want to be responsible for influencing the way that you're regarding this case," she told her partner.

"Too late," Jefferson said honestly. "I think we view this guy in the same exact light. There's just something there, something beneath the surface," he admitted as they walked from the building to her car in the parking lot. "The guy just gives me the creeps—and you have nothing to do with that."

Cheyenne eyed him doubtfully. "You would have thought of that on your own?"

Jefferson knew she didn't mean that the way that it sounded. He did his best not to take offense. "I'm a former Marine and a trained investigator. So yes. I most definitely would have thought of this on my own, even without your help, although it's nice to have you agree with me."

The lecture hall was filling up quickly around him, but Murphy was preoccupied, hardly noticing the students who were filing in. His mind was elsewhere, engaged in planning his next move—and the way he would savor the results.

That witch had it coming to her, he told himself, even more than the others he had eliminated over the last year and a half or so. He couldn't recall feeling this degree of excitement since he had managed to drain the last breath of air out of his aunt Lily's body. But that, she decided, was actually a good thing, because if this feeling had been a regular occurrence, then it definitely wouldn't have felt as special as it did—and he needed that feeling. It was feeding his soul.

The phrase made him laugh to himself.

Waiting to do this ate away at his patience, but it also felt exceedingly rewarding at the same time, the lecturer thought.

His eyes scanned the rows before him. Wouldn't his students be surprised at the double life he led.?

Murphy fingered the business cards tucked away in his pocket. His mouth curved ever so slightly as he smiled to himself. Fulfillment was a mere heart-beat away.

Or it would be very soon.

The overhead bell went off, signaling the beginning of the hour as well as class. Murphy pulled his shoulders back.

Time to perform again, the lecturer told himself.

"Settle down, people," he told them in a harsh, authoritarian voice.

And because the students mostly belonged to an older generation and actually rejoiced over the opportunity to be able to wedge their studies into what could be perceived as the little free time that they had, even at this late date in their lives, they complied.

Murphy scanned the area, taking everyone he saw into view. Ordinarily, he would have been looking for his next victim. There were a lot of candidates for him to choose from, he would have ordinarily thought. However, after meeting that police detective, the search had suddenly been abandoned. At least for the time being.

The policewoman would be the perfect candidate, he told himself. The fact actually put him in a rare good mood.

He could even feel his mouth curving.

"All right, who can tell me the significance of the passage that I assigned to you the last time we were together?"

A sea of hands shot up, eagerly seeking his attention, which to Murphy meant that his students were looking for his approval.

It made him smile.

It was a chilling smile to the students in the first few rows.

"Do you feel like having a drink?" Cheyenne asked Jefferson as they pulled up into her driveway a few minutes after they had left the scene of Aurora Valley College.

"I wouldn't mind. But I'm surprised that you're the one who's suggesting it," her partner told her. "He get to you that much?"

Cheyenne wanted to deny it, but in all honesty, she knew she really couldn't. Because the truth of it was, the lecturer actually *had* gotten to her. There was something completely unnerving about the man. It wasn't anything she could even put into words—it was just a feeling that was eating away at her.

A gut feeling so to speak, Cheyenne thought. She was convinced that the lecturer had something to do with his student's disappearance. There was just something in his eyes. Something cold and unnerving. It wasn't anything that she could even cite, or have been able to bring up in court.

It was something that just *was*.

Jeff got out of the car. He appeared to be choosing his words with care, aware that if he said the wrong thing, it would wind up setting Cheyenne off, and he definitely didn't want to do that. He just wanted

Cheyenne to understand that he was concerned about her. They were in the business of capturing "the bad guys" and he knew that.

He definitely didn't want "the bad guy" capturing her.

And since he had found himself falling for his partner, he was doubly wary about her safety and he *knew* that saying anything to that effect could very well set the woman off. He knew that he needed to tread very lightly here.

"Personally, I think that having a drink might not be such a bad idea," he told Cheyenne, watching her face.

"Just to be clear, I don't want you to think I'm looking to drink myself numb or senseless," she told him.

He raised his hands as if he was attesting to his innocence in the matter. "Never even crossed my mind."

She nodded. "Okay, just so we're clear. But you do agree with me, right? There is something about that man that just makes your flesh all but curl up and want to creep away."

Jefferson nodded his agreement at her words. "Oh, absolutely—in double time," her partner told her, stifling a shiver.

"But we can't drink on an empty stomach," Cheyenne pointed out. "Tell you what, I'll make dinner for us and then we can decide whether or not we want to cap off the evening with a drink."

Jefferson's eyes crinkled as he smiled at her.

"That's not exactly the way I was thinking of capping off the evening."

Cheyenne smiled, her eyes crinkling. "We'll talk about that, too," she told him. "But first we eat."

Jefferson inclined his head, then gave his partner a smart salute. He refrained from hugging her, although he really wanted to.

"Fine with me," he told her as they walked into the kitchen, "but I have to admit that I do feel guilty, making you do all this work. I can still order something in for us," he told her.

Cheyenne put her hands on her hips. "Do you hear me complaining?"

"Well, no, I don't. But—" he started to tell her only to have Cheyenne cut into his words to put a stop to his protest before it could get underway.

"No, no buts, Jefferson," Cheyenne informed her partner. "All I want from you is to have you just sit and wait—and eat your dinner once it's ready for you," she ordered her partner.

And then with that, she turned her attention to preparing dinner.

Chapter 24

Cheyenne couldn't shake the feeling that she was being watched. It had been going on for several days now. Evenings, actually.

Admittedly, it was nothing she could really put her finger on, but the feeling just seemed to cling to her nonetheless. It had nothing to do with the way that Jeff was looking at her. They had been sharing dinners now whenever they could—and breakfasts as well.

Tonight, after dinner was over—and surprisingly he had volunteered to help her with the dishes—they had gone into her bedroom to enjoy some much-deserved "alone" time—together.

But although she responded to him more and more, Cheyenne couldn't sufficiently relax enough to enjoy herself with him this time, not the way she had previous times.

Holding her in his arms, Jeff sensed that something was off this time. He drew back and looked at the woman he had come to not only have a great deal of respect for, but growing affection toward as well.

As a matter of fact, he felt as if he was in love with her. He just didn't want to admit it to her as of yet because he was afraid that he would wind up scaring her off. He had been taught to tread lightly in everything he did, which was what he intended on doing until he felt he could safely proceed and take the next step.

She felt almost as stiff as a board in his arms. "What's the matter?" Jefferson finally asked her.

His question took her by surprise. She had been trying so hard to act as if everything was all right. Cheyenne glanced at him quizzically. "What makes you think that there's something the matter?" she asked Jefferson, doing her best to feign innocence.

Jefferson frowned ever so slightly. "Because I'm not an idiot. Because I've gotten to know you quite well in a short amount of time and because I can just feel it in my gut. And yes, you aren't the only one with gut feelings. Now, talk to me, Cheyenne," her partner urged. "What has you looking as if you're anticipating having something explode on you? What's wrong?"

Cheyenne raised her chin a little. "Nothing's wrong," she insisted flatly.

Jefferson blew out a breath as he leaned back against the headboard, looking at her. "You know, I think we should mark this date down on the calendar. This is the first time that you've lied to me. Unless, of course, I was so enamored with you that I was totally blind to the first time that you lied to me."

Cheyenne sighed, tucking herself into the space that was created against Jefferson's body by his arm. "No, there was no 'first time' before this one," she admitted honestly. With a soulful sigh, she turned her entire body into Jefferson's and looked up at his face. "I'm sorry. It's just that I can't seem to get away from the feeling that I'm being watched."

Jeff honestly wasn't expecting that and thought maybe he had misunderstood what she was saying. "Do you mean that *we're* being watched?"

Cheyenne shook her head with feeling. "No, just me," she told him. Sitting up in bed, she pulled her knees up against her and leaned her chin on them. "I know that I'm being foolish and most likely I'm just imagining things, but I still can't seem to shake the feeling that there's someone watching me. That feeling is holding me pretty tightly in its grip." She sighed, looking at the man next to her. "You probably think I'm crazy or, best-case scenario, just imagining things."

"Are you kidding? I've got a great deal of respect for the legendry Cavanaugh 'gut.' If you feel like you're being watched, then that feeling deserves to be explored," Jefferson said in all seriousness.

Cheyenne regarded him with abject wonder, as well as with huge secret relief. "You're serious," she cried in astonishment.

"Of course I'm serious," he told her. "Why wouldn't I be?" her partner asked. And then he added, "We've already slept together a number of times—all glorious, I might add. And I'm not attempting to convince you to do anything or to weaponize anything to use to my advantage. In case you haven't figured it out yet, I'm not that kind of guy. For what's going on between us to really progress, it needs to progress with honesty."

Cheyenne nodded at him, her manner turning exceedingly friendly. The man was being honest, she thought as joy slithered though her. Very honest. "You know, that realization is beginning to dawn on me."

"Well, I'm very glad to hear that," Jeff told her. His mind cast about for ways to get her to unwind and relax. "How would you feel about watching some TV, or doing something else to relax? Or, if you're really being haunted by that feeling that there's someone watching us, I could just stand guard, keeping an eye out on you and you could get some much-needed rest," he suggested.

Cheyenne looked at him in complete speechless wonder. "You'd do that for me?" she questioned her partner.

Jefferson's smile was compelling. "Of course I'd do that."

"You wouldn't report me to some authority on the

premises, or tell some higher-up that I was asking for preferential treatment?" she asked.

He laughed at the suggestion. "You're a Cavanaugh. Who am I going to report you to? And for that matter, who would believe me?"

She smiled at him. "I'm not about to abuse my so-called 'power,'" she informed him with a touch of indignity.

Her partner chuckled. "Good to know," he told her. With that, he took Cheyenne back into his arms.

She savored the warmth of his body penetrating hers and for a moment said nothing. And then she looked up at him. "Jeff?"

"Yes?" he asked, glancing down into her face as he held her close against him.

"Could I change my answer?" she asked him.

He wasn't following her. "Your answer about what?"

"My answer about making love with you right now," she explained.

Jeff grinned broadly into her face, a face he was finding himself falling for extremely quickly and extremely harder every passing day. "If you're up for a do-over, so am I—as long as you don't worry that that whoever is watching you is about to get one hell of an eyeful."

She laughed, tickled as she waved the thought away. And, with any luck, waved it totally out of existence.

"That is the creep's problem, not mine," Cheyenne informed her partner, making a nebulous reference to whoever might be watching the two of them. She turned her body into his.

Cheyenne found that she really appreciated her partner being this thoughtful toward her. Appreciated the fact that he wasn't telling her that she was imagining things, or that all of this existed just in her head. Those sort of assertions would have just made her furious.

It would have also made her feel abandoned. Jeff cutting her this slack just made her unsettled feelings that much easier for her to cope with and she was really grateful to him for that.

"Come here," she coaxed. "The embers under my fire just might wind up going out if you don't make up your mind to feed them in the next few minutes," Cheyenne warned her partner with a broad wink.

"We wouldn't want that," Jeff told her, bringing his mouth down to hers.

Within moments, Cheyenne's partner was getting lost in her lips.

Murphy's breathing grew labored as he watched the two performers going through their motions. He had his binoculars trained on the pair and had, patiently, for a while now.

He was positioned in a hiding place in a house across the street. The people whose house this was were on vacation, so for all intents and purposes, the house he was using was abandoned.

Anger creased his features. The witch was doing

this just to control the detective, the lecturer thought. The bitch had no shame to her. There was certainly nothing straightforward or even a drop of innocence about her, Murphy thought angrily.

He could feel tension sharply lancing through his body. He savored the anticipation of being able to bring her down—and it would be soon, he promised himself.

Very, very soon.

The first time he could get these two so-called detectives to separate so that he could make his move, he would, the man promised himself. And it was going to be a good one. That detective would pay for that high-and-mighty attitude she was projecting and for parading around controlling the men surrounding her.

Just like Aunt Lily had done, he thought bitterly, remembering the taste of death as life flowed away through his hands and out of his victim's body.

The very thought made his nostrils flare. He savored the anticipation of what was to come. Savored the thought of making it happen.

Soon.

Very, very soon, the college lecturer promised himself.

Despite her very strong common sense, Cheyenne had to admit that she couldn't completely eliminate that uneasy feeling that seemed to be haunting her every move. It haunted her even during their lovemaking and the time that came after that.

It was there, in the background, during every waking minute she was aware of.

In the morning, after Cheyenne had made them both breakfast, she had decided that for a change of pace, her partner needed to go to his place to get a change of clothing. They agreed that they would go into the precinct separately.

"Most likely, if they're paying any attention, the members of our team are undoubtedly talking about us being an item," she told Jefferson. "But there's no reason for us to hurry that along more than we need to at the moment."

"Cheyenne, these are trained investigators," he pointed out to her as he made his way to the door. "If they're really speculating about the situation between us, how long do you think that we can actually fool them?"

"At least for a little while," she said. "Longer if they're being polite. Tell you what, let's just take this one step at a time."

Jeff paused to take her into his arms and kiss her goodbye. "One step at a time it is," he promised, repeating what she had said to him earlier. "I'll see you in the office in a little while."

Cheyenne nodded. "You've got it, stranger," she told him with a laugh. "I've got a few things to clean up here and then I plan on heading out to the precinct."

He nodded as he walked out of her house. "Sounds

like a plan to me," Jefferson said just before he closed the front door behind him.

The man really brought a smile to her face, Cheyenne couldn't help thinking, a warm feeling stirring all through her.

"C'mon, Chey, get a move on," she instructed herself. "You haven't done a single thing around this place for days now. For all you know, you might not get another chance to do anything for another few days more. There's dust around here celebrating an anniversary."

Saying that, Cheyenne grabbed a dust rag and got busy, starting to move it around the area that was all but begging for a cleanup—or at least seemed to be begging for one in her eyes.

Because she had to get to her place of work, she moved quickly, running the vacuum cleaner with one hand and moving the dust rag with the other. Cheyenne was so busy, trying to get the job done as quickly as possible, that she wound up being oblivious to everything else.

Speed to her was of the essence. She had to get to the precinct as quickly as she possibly could. She had the feeling that she and Jefferson were onto something. They suspected that smug lecturer no matter what he'd said to try to dissuade them from doing so. She wanted to dig into the man's records as well as into his students' records. Something might just lead them in the right direction.

While she knew that coincidences did happen,

something in her gut made her feel that this was way too much of one. Jon Murphy had had at least three of the missing older women attending his classes. That just didn't seem possible.

Granted it could have just "happened" that way, but why would it? she couldn't help wondering. This was not a tiny college. Could the missing women have more in common than just being missing? And if so, what was it?

There was no time like the present to find out, she told herself. As soon as she and Jeff got in, she wanted to check a few things out and then she and her partner were going to make their way to the college to talk to administrators who knew the lecturer.

Maybe she and Jefferson were barking up the wrong tree, as it were.

Shutting off the vacuum cleaner, Cheyenne turned around to lean it against the wall.

Startled, she wound up dropping the appliance on the floor.

Murphy was standing in her living room.

Cheyenne's eyebrows immediately drew together in anger. She knew instinctively that she couldn't display even a hint of fear to this man despite the fact that her heart was slamming against her chest so hard right now, it was all but creating a hole where it hit.

She immediately thought of her weapon. It had been locked up last night and was still locked away. She needed to get her hands on it, if only to make him back away—although she sensed that the man was a great deal more dangerous than he had initially been given credit for.

"What are you doing here, Professor Murphy?" Cheyenne asked, the sheer anger in her eyes holding him back.

The smile on his lips was cold and absolutely bone-chilling. "What do you think I'm doing here?"

"Invading my space without an invitation," Cheyenne snapped at him. "I'll thank you to get out of here."

"I will, when I've done what I've come here to do," he told her, taking measured steps toward her.

"No," she told him firmly. "You will go *now*," Cheyenne ordered him.

The eerie smile on Murphy's face continued as he took another step toward her. "You sound pretty brave for a woman with only a few more minutes to live," he informed her icily.

Chapter 25

Cheyenne knew she had to keep the man who had broken into her house talking until she could figure out a way to get her hands on her weapon and make him back away. The really odd thing was that she was about to actually go get her weapon when her attention had been diverted to vacuuming her floors and rugs instead. Had she put that off, even for a short while, she would have already been armed when the lecturer had broken into her house the way he had.

"How did you know where I lived?" Cheyenne demanded, hostility echoing in her voice as she tried to divert his attention.

The expression on the lecturer's face was filled with sheer anger and hostility. "Oh come on, give me some credit, Detective Cavanaugh." Murphy smirked as he talked down to her. "You're not the only one who knows how to track a person down."

Murphy took another step toward her, managing to crowd her into a small space against the wall. "This is the part where I tell you that if you don't fight this too hard, it won't hurt you as much." His mouth curved as an ugly expression took over his face. "But we both know that isn't true. Personally, I hope you *do* fight this. You know, seeing you struggle with fear radiating from your eyes would be a great deal more rewarding for me than having you crumble in front of me and just give up." He leered at her in anticipation. "That part will come later."

What Cheyenne heard in his voice made her blood run cold. Cheyenne grabbed a small metal statue of an eagle that was in the middle of the end table closest to her. With a bloodcurdling scream, she threw the statue, pitching it right at Murphy. She managed to hit the man square in the face.

The lecturer shrieked in pain. Running a hand over his face, he looked down at it and saw that there was blood on his palm and fingers.

Fury entered his eyes.

"Oh, you're going to pay for that, you bitch," he promised, savoring every syllable that he uttered. "Pay big-time!"

Cheyenne did what she could to project complete and nonchalant defiance.

"Big-time?" she repeated with a sneer. "You mean even more than just being killed?" she asked, showing Murphy how patently absurd that claim of his had sounded to her.

Jon Murphy's expression turned menacing and looked even uglier than it already had. He wanted to see even more fear evident in her face, but all he could see was defiance there—and that fact completely enraged him.

"I am going to kill you by inches, bitch!" Murphy promised viciously, shouting the words almost into her face. "You hear me? Bloody inches!"

"You know, I think that it's safe to say that the neighbors heard you," Cheyenne told him, doing what she could to bait the man.

Cutting the distance between them short, Murphy made a dive for her. At the last minute, Cheyenne managed to kick the lecturer, delivering the blow dead center to his stomach, then another to his genitals. She knocked the air right out of him.

The killer tried to catch her and made a grab for her throat, but Cheyenne managed to twist out of his reach at the very last moment.

She had the presence of mind to make her way over to the cabinet where she always kept her weapon locked up. She knew that she somehow needed to get the cabinet open in order to get at her handgun.

Murphy made another grab for her, trying to get hold of her waist. Again, Cheyenne succeeded in eluding the serial killer's grasp, just managing to duck out of his reach.

Her heart slammed against her chest. It almost

hurt in its intensity this time. She knew that if Murphy—or whatever his actual name was—managed to get his hands on her, that very well might spell the end of her. He had a look in his eyes that was absolutely frightening. Hardened killers had that sort of look about them.

Murphy managed to twist around again, reaching for her as he cursed her viciously.

Damn but she really wished she hadn't been so conscientious about locking up her weapon. After all, she mocked herself, who was going to break into her house just to get their hands on her gun? Right now, she was the one who needed to get her hands on her gun, not some theoretical stranger, Cheyenne thought in frustration.

Eluding the maniacal lecturer's grasping hands, Cheyenne twisted and turned, managing to continue getting away from Murphy as he continued to keep trying to grab her.

She could see that she was making the lecturer furious.

"You're just fighting the inevitable, you stupid bitch," he said, taunting her. "The more you fight, the more I'm going to really enjoy squeezing the very life out of you," he promised her nastily. "Bit by bit. Just like with Aunt Lily."

She wanted to ask him who this "Aunt Lily" person was, but this was not the time to get that information out of him. She could do that once he was handcuffed in front of her.

Just then, as Murphy was about to make another grab for her, uttering yet another bloodcurdling yell, Cheyenne's front door suddenly flew open. The impact made it bang loudly against the back wall. The doorknob left a slight hole in the wall where it had made contact.

Caught completely by surprise, the lecturer swung around and stared at this newest development.

His mouth dropped open.

Murphy continued to watch the person who had just come rushing in.

"You!" he spat when he realized that it was the police detective's partner who had just rushed into the house. "So now it's officially a party," Murphy declared with a nasty, laugh.

Murphy saw the gun that was in the police detective's hand. His scowling face darkened even more.

"You can't shoot me," the lecturer sneered at McDougall's face. "I'm unarmed," he pointed out, reveling in the fact that he was correct.

It was just the minor distraction that she needed, Cheyenne thought. Propelling herself forward, she made a grab for Murphy's arm. She twisted it as hard as she could, moving it behind the lecturer's back.

Murphy screamed in pain.

"You certainly look unarmed, but that still won't save you," Cheyenne told him, thoroughly enjoying being able to strike at least a little fear into the man's heart.

In her view, it was nothing short of payback. As

a matter of fact, she had to exercise extreme control to keep from breaking Murphy's arm. In her heart, she felt that she would have been completely justified if she had. But she also knew that that wasn't what she and the other agents of law enforcement were all about.

There was the slightest bit of hesitation on Cheyenne's part and Murphy instantly attempted to use that to his advantage. Lunging, he grabbed the gun that her partner had drawn when he'd entered Cheyenne's house and taken in what was going on.

The lecturer tried to shoot at Jefferson but wound up missing the man because Cheyenne's partner had ducked.

For her part, Cheyenne made a grab for the same eagle statue she had previously thrown at the lecturer. Holding on to it by its base, she swung the statue at the lecturer as hard as she could and managed to hit Murphy in the back of his head.

She'd brought the lecturer down before he could do any harm to her partner or to her.

Dusting herself off, Cheyenne looked down at the unconscious man. A feeling of triumph washed over her. She couldn't help smiling.

Breathing hard, she told her partner with satisfaction, "I believe that this is what is referred to as 'checkmate.'"

She allowed herself one precious moment, after looking over to assure herself that the lecturer was indeed really out, to throw herself into her partner's arms. And then she hugged him for all she was worth.

"What made you come back?" she asked her partner, amazed at how close she had come to actually meeting her end. The same, she knew, could be said for Jefferson.

She had naturally assumed that her partner had left for the apartment where he was staying so he could get a change of clothes. That would have taken him some time and she could have been dead before he'd finished.

"The answer to that is really funny. I realized that I had walked off with your keys instead of taking mine," he told her, holding up the keys for her benefit. "When I tried putting the key into the ignition, the key actually fit, which was the strange part, but then it refused to turn. After two attempts, when I couldn't get the car to start up, I realized that I had picked up your keys instead of mine by accident. What threw me," he continued, "was that the key did fit into the ignition, which was highly unusual."

Cheyenne's eyes fluttered shut for a second as she thought of how close she had come to her own demise. And then they flew open again. She was sincerely grateful that there had been such a mix-up.

"Thank God for mistakes," she said to her partner in all sincerity. "I honestly believe that this guy would have just as happily killed me as looked at me."

Jeff had learned something that he hadn't had a

chance to share with his partner as of yet. "This scum and his sickening killings have been making the rounds on all the podcast shows recently," he told Cheyenne. "Seems that this serial killer took a great deal of joy in killing strong-willed women, and 'strong-willed woman' definitely describes you to a tee," Jefferson pointed out.

Just then, the lecturer moaned. He was regaining consciousness. When he turned his eyes toward Cheyenne, there was nothing short of sheer contempt and hatred in them. When he spoke, he sounded almost maniacal.

"You haven't escaped me, Aunt Lily," he told her angrily. "You're going to die. If it's the last thing I do, I'm going to kill you. You're going to pay for what you did to me. Pay dearly, do you hear?"

Cheyenne eyed her partner. "Well, that solves that mystery," she told Jeff with finality. "I guess the other victims reminded Murphy of his aunt Lily, too."

"Don't talk about her!" Murphy shrieked at the woman he had taken a vehement dislike to. And then he spat, "You're not fit to even say her name."

Cheyenne exchanged looks with her partner. "He definitely has a problem, and we," she went on with a satisfied, relieved smile, "definitely have the serial killer we were looking for."

"Nothing! You have nothing!" Murphy fairly shrieked at Cheyenne, his expression looking as if he wanted to vivisect her. The next second, he managed to knock her out of the way and hurdled himself at Jefferson. Grabbing his throat, he knocked Cheyenne's partner's head against the floor.

For a second, Jefferson looked as if he had passed out. Frightened, Cheyenne clawed the lecturer away, digging her nails into Murphy's face. She was determined to separate the man from her partner in any way that she possibly could.

The man was going to hurt Jefferson over her dead body, Cheyenne promised herself.

The lecturer tried to fight her off, but a surge of almost superhuman strength surged through Cheyenne, helping her keep the man at bay.

She knew it wouldn't last.

Just in time, Jefferson came to. He wrestled the lecturer away from Cheyenne and bent the man's arms behind his back really hard.

"Cuff him, Cheyenne," Jeff ordered his partner at the exact same time that Murphy shrieked in pain.

Cheyenne managed to straighten up just as her partner dragged Murphy to his feet. He decided to put the cuffs on the serial killer himself.

"Call backup," Jefferson instructed Cheyenne, referring to the precinct. "This guy isn't going to let up until he winds up killing one of us, if not both. We need to get backup here."

Breathing hard, Cheyenne started to place the call to the precinct. With a guttural yell, Murphy threw himself at her partner, pointing his gun at Jefferson.

It all happened so fast, it seemed like one huge blur. Murphy began to aim his gun at her partner and Cheyenne swung up her hand, shooting the lecturer. Murphy went down in a bloody heap, screaming in pain.

He was dead as he hit the floor.

Cheyenne fell back, exhausted and breathless, never taking her eyes off the man. She couldn't believe he was dead.

But the lecturer's eyes remained lifeless as they stared upward. His face was pale.

Relieved, Cheyenne all but collapsed into her partner's arms. "I think we're finally safe," she cried.

"If we're not, then this creep belongs to the breed of the undead," her partner told her. Holding Cheyenne to him with one arm while watching the prone man on the floor, Jeff placed a call to the nearby EMT.

Giving the driver directions on how to get there, he continued looking at Cheyenne. When he ended the call, he told his partner that the driver would be there to pick up the serial killer's body very soon.

The nightmare, at least for now, was finally over.

"If anything ever called for a celebration, it's this," Andrew Cavanaugh declared the following afternoon as paperwork was being filed and all the i's were dotted and the t's were crossed. The former chief of police looked around at the members of the department who were surrounding him as the announcement was made that the serial killer who had been plaguing the city was finally dead. "I know what you're thinking," Andrew said. "We just had one.

But our newest detective from Texas, working with his partner, my very stubborn niece, just managed to take a serial killer out of circulation and that deserves acknowledgment. Big-time. Besides, this'll give me a chance to cook," he said with a wink. "I like evening the score."

"After all these years, it's a competition?" Brian asked his brother in surprise.

"It's always been a competition," Andrew said with another wink.

Cheyenne turned toward her partner. "Welcome to the family," she told him with an amused laugh. She was unbelievably grateful that this was finally over and that it had ended the way that it had.

Standing amid the others, Jefferson looked at her in surprise. And then, as her words sank in, his expression changed, warming. "You mean that?"

She detected an undercurrent in his words. Well, she had come this far, she might as well say the rest of it. "I do if you want me to," she told him.

Brian walked up between them, putting one hand on each of their shoulders. "Say yes," he encouraged Jefferson, adding, "Cheyenne probably doesn't want this to be public knowledge but she was engaged to a guy who wanted her to move to the East Coast with him. When she refused to go because it would mean leaving everything she knew behind, he broke off the engagement and just walked out on her. This—" he gestured toward Cheyenne "—is the happiest the family has seen Cheyenne in six months."

"Uncle Brian," Cheyenne protested with a warning note in her voice.

Brian shrugged. "Well, it's true," he said pointedly. "Go home," he ordered the detectives who were in his office, then added, "Rest up for the next case." And then the chief of detectives smiled broadly. "We get our rest whenever we can get it," he reminded the others.

"Sounds like a good suggestion to me," Cheyenne told her partner.

"And I know just the way I'd like to relax," Jefferson said, his eyes meeting hers.

She leaned her head in toward his, whispering, "Your place or mine?"

"Doesn't matter as long as we're together," Jefferson told her in all honesty as they and the others all filed out of the chief of d's office.

"You're serious?" she asked, looking up at her partner.

"I've learned never to lie to my partner," he told her as he grinned. "You taught me that."

Her eyes were smiling at him. "You're a good learner," she told him.

"I'd like to think so," Jefferson answered.

"So, we'll be getting together this weekend in order to celebrate getting this guy off the streets and ultimately into a coffin?" Andrew asked as he followed his niece and her partner out. He had been invited to the precinct expressly for this announcement.

"All right then, we will be there with bells on," Cheyenne promised.

"With something else on as well, I hope," one of her brothers, walking out behind them, said with a laugh.

Jefferson gave his partner's brother a censoring look. "I'd say speak for yourself, but it would probably get me in trouble," he laughed, avoiding her brother's smirking look.

With one arm tucked around Cheyenne's waist, he ushered his partner toward the elevator. The best, he knew, was yet to come.

Because tonight, Jefferson promised himself, he was planning to set the stage to ask Cheyenne to marry him. Their life together would truly begin from that point on and he, for one, could hardly wait for that to happen.

Epilogue

Andrew didn't usually scan the internet news sources on his computer for his daily information. But he was short on time today, so he had decided to indulge his curiosity this one time, especially since it would be a quick perusal just to get the highlights.

The internet had just been coming into fruition when he had wound up resigning his position as the chief of police in Aurora in order to take care of his children.

He definitely hadn't expected to stumble across anything of interest. And yet, he did.

The headline caught his attention immediately.

His mouth fell open as he read. As did the sick feeling in the pit of his stomach.

Is there another serial killer lurking in Aurora's shadows?

Have we really seen the last of the serial killer who had been terrorizing the good people of Aurora? We were told that he was dead, but maybe we have all been lied to. Or worse yet, maybe the serial killer has come back from the dead to avenge himself on the unsuspecting citizens of this fair city. A body mutilated in the exact same manner as with the first wave of executions was found just on the edge of the Santa Ana Freeway in the center of Aurora.

I would seriously advise the people of Aurora to exercise extreme caution and be very, very careful when they venture out of their homes.

Andrew frowned, curling his hands against his thighs in frustration—another thing about reading stories on the internet that he found extremely annoying. Had he been reading this article in a local newspaper, he would have now had the satisfying pleasure of tearing the pages out of the newspaper and then shredding those same pages into teeny-tiny unreadable confetti.

He couldn't do that with what he read on the screen. Not unless he printed the pages first and then tore them up. It seemed to him like a colossal waste of ink and paper, doing that.

"What mindless nonsense," Andrew grumbled. As far as he was concerned, this article was just a piece of sensationalism. It was merely meant to drum fear into the local citizens' hearts. There was no other reason for this article to exist. "They should be ashamed of themselves," he declared angrily.

"Who are you talking to, dear?" Rose asked her husband as she walked into the room. "Who should be ashamed of themselves?" she asked. And then her eyes narrowed as she saw that the usually dormant laptop was on and open to a news site.

This was a highly unusual situation, Rose thought, given that there wasn't a recipe being highlighted on the screen. She frowned, drawing closer and reading. Her eyes weren't what they used to be.

Andrew was not given to using the internet for random searches. If he wanted to find out something about someone, he would call them or get in contact with that person the tradition way—by driving over and dropping by.

"Andrew, what's going on?" she asked her husband, concerned. "Is there something wrong?"

He wasn't about to lie to Rose, even to spare his wife the worry and concern that mentioning something like this—the appearance of another serial killer—would wind up generating. If he made something up, it just wouldn't work.

Ever since they had first gotten married, Rose could always see right through him if he wasn't being completely truthful with her.

"Possibly," he said, answering her question regarding something being wrong.

Rose blew out a breath as she shook her head. "English, Andrew. Speak English," his wife told him.

"I can't help you if I don't have a clue what you're saying."

Andrew sighed. He *really* didn't want to pull her into this. Waving his hand at his words, he told her, "Forget I said anything."

But his wife shook her head rather emphatically. "I'm afraid that it's too late for that, Andrew. All right, my love. Time to come clean."

Andrew sighed. He was beginning to believe that years of living a rather laidback, sedate life, helping him prepare the complex menus he had become known for had gotten to his wife. Rather than Rose getting a hobby for herself or something along those lines, his quiet, reasonable, loving wife had suddenly taken a second look at the sort of life her husband had led before he had resigned his position and found herself longing for a more exciting life than the one she was now leading.

Andrew slanted a look in Rose's direction. She appeared intensely focused on what he was about to say. He knew in his heart that she would give him no peace until he answered her question.

Truthfully.

"It looks as if that serial killer that Cheyenne and Jefferson took down either had a groupie bent on following in his footsteps, or some other twisted human being was hoping to drum up the sort of 'hero worship' the original killer had generated.

"In other words, according to this article I found on the internet, someone is attempting to emulate that sick serial killer and has left a body, killed in the same fashion, on the edge of the freeway." Andrew gestured toward the yellow pad next to the computer that he had been writing on. "I wrote down the location where the body was found and I intend to give it to Brian so he can send out some of his people to check it out."

He sighed, looking at the pad. "This could all be a tempest in a teapot, or it could very possibly be round two of the worst serial killer the city of Aurora has ever seen." Andrew raised his eyebrows as he pinned down his wife. "Satisfied?"

Rose shook her head. "No, I'm not—and I won't be until this so-called serial killer wannabe is behind bars—or made to pay the ultimate price for what he has done and for what he intends to do."

"Much as I would like to, sweetheart, we can't get ahead of ourselves and arrest this slime for his future crimes," Andrew told his wife. "But arresting this mad dog will stop him from committing those future murders."

Rose nodded. "I'll buy that. Have you told the family that you suspect that there's a serial killer wannabe roaming around our city?"

Andrew shook his head. "No, not yet. I just stumbled across this article on the internet—just before you walked in on me."

Rose pressed her lips together thoughtfully. "Well, dear, I think I have the theme for your next party— or at least the excuse for it," she said with a smile, winking at Andrew.

"A supposed serial killer lurking in the shadows isn't exactly something to celebrate, Rose," the former chief of police told his wife.

"No, it isn't," Rose agreed. "But getting him off the streets and behind bars certainly is," his wife told him. She paused to kiss Andrew's lips with feeling.

Andrew chuckled. "Well, I certainly can't argue with that," he agreed.

He felt as if he was finally able to release the monster that was living and growing inside of him—and it was really such a huge relief to do that. He had been living with these fantasies for so long.

And then, when he had read about that college lecturer, the one the article had said was killing women who resembled and reminded him of his aunt, something within him had just snapped. He had no aunt that had made his life miserable, no aunt that he wanted to destroy, over and over again. No aunt at all, or family for that matter, really.

Ever since he could remember, he had been making his way from foster home to cold, lonely foster home, all the while picking up basic survival tactics.

Because he had a slight build until he reached the age of seventeen, he had been picked on and belittled over and over again, dreaming of the day he would be able to get his revenge on his tormentors.

And then, miraculously, he'd had a growth spurt— a really *big* growth spurt—and the kids weren't picking on him anymore. What they did do was avoid making any eye contact with him at all, hoping that he would forget that they had tormented him.

But he didn't forget.

He didn't forget one single moment of their ridicule. Not one single display of cruelty that they had sent his way.

He had patience.

He could wait to get his revenge.

Waiting just made it that much sweeter when the moment of revenge finally materialized.

And then, when he had read that article about the serial killer that had lived right here, lived among them completely undetected, something inside him had suddenly blossomed. It felt as if his way had just been highlighted for him and he knew just what he needed to do to achieve his ultimate revenge for all those years he had suffered.

He would get his revenge and strike fear into all those worthless hearts that had made his life so miserable for so long.

He would show them, he promised himself. He would show them all.

He savored the thought.

And he had already started his journey, he thought with glee. His jaw hardened, remembering.

Make fun of him, would they?

Belittle him, would they?

Well, he'd show them. He'd show them all, he silently promised himself.

All he needed was a coherent plan to kill all the

people he had been forced to cohabitate with when he had been a young boy in the foster system.

He closed his eyes, envisioning it all. A wave of glee mixed with anticipation washed over him, sending shivers all up and down his spine.

His hands grew damp as he envisioned how he planned to get even. And the marks he planned to leave in their flesh.

He couldn't wait until he was able to put his plan in motion.

Opening his laptop, he typed in the name of the man he wanted to be his second victim.

In order for that to come about, he needed to find Glen Shaffer's address.

Locating the man was a lot simpler than he would have thought. He congratulated himself as he stared at the address.

"I hope you have your affairs in order, Glen," he told the name on the screen, laughing in anticipation. "Because you don't have much time left to do that, you worthless waste of human flesh. When I'm finished with you, you'll wish that you had never been born. Just the way you made me feel," he said angrily between teeth that were clenched so hard, they threatened to break if he exerted any more pressure on them.

And then, suddenly, he smiled in anticipation.

* * * * *

*Available now from
Harlequin Romantic Suspense!*

Get 3 FREE REWARDS!

We'll send you 2 FREE Books plus a FREE Mystery Gift.

FREE Value Over **$20**

Both the **Harlequin Intrigue®** and **Harlequin® Romantic Suspense** series feature compelling novels filled with heart-racing action-packed romance that will keep you on the edge of your seat.